A
Bride
For
Keegan

By Linda Shenton

Matchett

A Bride for Keegan
By Linda Shenton Matchett

Cover Design: V. McKevitt
Author photo by: Wes Matchett

ISBN-13: 978-1-7363256-4-3

Published by Shortwave Press

Chapter One

Fiona Quigley swallowed and pressed her hands against her middle hoping her breakfast wouldn't reappear. The rocking of the train might be soothing to some, but the incessant swaying made the contents of her stomach swirl. Her approaching destination added to her belly's distress. She licked her lips in an effort to bring moisture to her dry mouth. In for a penny, in for a pound as Mama was wont to say.

Unbidden tears filled Fiona's eyes, and she blinked them away. Her choices had been limited. Who was she kidding? They were nonexistent. Hence, being trapped on a train hurtling across the continent.

"Are you all right, dearie?"

Sliding her gaze from the blurred scenery outside the soot-encrusted window to the buxom woman across the aisle, she forced a smile and nodded. "I will be once I'm on solid ground, Mrs. Marcussen. 'Tis nothing that can be done until then. How are you faring?"

The elderly widow reached over and patted her hand. "Perfectly fine. I've got a sturdy constitution. Not like the late Mr. Marcussen. He suffered as you do." She tittered. "The poor man could barely ride a horse without feeling queasy. It's the way for some. Hopefully, your ride from the station to your new home won't be far."

"I'm fine in a wagon or carriage. 'Tis just trains that cause distress." Fiona sighed. And marrying complete strangers. Sure, she'd exchanged some letters with Keegan O'Rourke, and he seemed like a lovely man, but how much did she really know him? He seemed to be a man of integrity and deep faith, but he'd insisted they wed by proxy before she headed to Des Moines. Was she an eejit for agreeing? All the mail-order brides she'd heard about met their prospective husbands before tying the knot.

Mrs. Marcussen grinned and waved her hand, sending the cloyingly sweet odor of her perfume toward Fiona. "Perhaps you're getting a case of cold feet. Not unusual for a bride, but from the description of your young man, you've nothing to fear."

"So it would appear."

"Didn't you tell me he included a letter of recommendation from his pastor?" The gray-haired woman tilted her head. "That must set your mind at ease."

"A bit. Thank you for your encouragement, Mrs. Marcussen, but I think I'd like to try to sleep for a bit." And pray. Pray that she wasn't making the biggest mistake of her life. Pray that Mama had been right in sending her from Boston into the rugged wilds of Iowa.

"Of course, dearie. I'll wake you in time to freshen up."

Fiona closed her eyes and leaned against the back of the seat. Blowing out a deep breath, she stretched her legs, glad that Keegan could afford a second-class seat for her. Not quite as luxurious as first class, with its plush chairs and carpeted floors, but comfortable nonetheless, and certainly not as crowded as third class. She shuddered. How did those people stand being crammed together like an Irish pub on St. Patrick's Day?

Dear God, help me be a good wife to Keegan, to love him as a wife should, like Mama and Papa loved each other—through thick and thin. Even when they had but a few pennies to rub together, they were happy. Until the war took him.

Her chin trembled. Mama was never the same after he died. The light in her eyes dimmed. Sure, she tried to hide her sadness from Fiona, but the distant gaze that had taken up permanent residence on her face told the truth. She looked forward to the time she could join him. And two weeks ago, she'd gotten her wish.

The doctors said it was cancer, but Fiona knew it was a broken heart. Taking care of her baby girl, as Mama insisted on calling her even at twenty-five, her mother had contacted a matrimonial agency to make arrangements. When Mama managed to find a Protestant Irishman, she'd declared it was a sign from God that Iowa was to be Fiona's new home. In a daze, she'd agreed to the plan, if only to make her mother's last days less stressful.

A muffled explosion sounded, and the whistle shrieked. Brakes squealed. She was thrown forward as the car lurched and shimmied on the tracks, her forehead hitting the seat in front of her. Pain exploded in her face as she fell to the floor in a heap. Cries and gasps from her fellow passengers filled the train. What was happening?

After what felt like hours, but was probably only minutes, the train came to a halt. Fiona cracked her eyelids and squinted toward the windows but steam enveloped the glass. Had some poor animal blocked the tracks forcing them to stop? No, there had been the blast. Shouts and gunshots sounded from outside.

Gunshots? Fiona's heart pounded. Apparently, Iowa was wilder than she anticipated.

Someone moaned beside her, and she turned. Mrs. Marcussen lay on the floor, a gash on her cheek. The woman's skin was ashen, and tears seeped from her eyes.

"Mrs. Marcussen." Fiona sat up, then closed her eyes and gulped when her vision swam. Her stomach quivered, and she swallowed against the nausea.

"M-Miss Quigley, what—"

Fiona cleared her throat and opened her eyes. "I don't know. Someone will come soon." She stroked the woman's shoulder. Where was her reticule? With a grunt, she rolled to her knees, then searched under her seat. She scooted her satchel to the side and spied the small drawstring bag wedged against the wall. Stretching her arm, her fingers wiggled, then managed to catch the ribbon. She tugged it toward herself, then opened the bag to retrieve her handkerchief.

Conversation mingled with cries. From the back of the car, a man's voice cut through the noise claiming he would get to the bottom of things.

"This may hurt a bit." Fiona pressed the linen against the older woman's cheek.

Mrs. Marcussen hissed in a breath.

"I'm sorry." She peeked under the hanky. "Hopefully, there's a doctor on the train. Your injury may need stitches."

The woman nodded. She made an attempt to sit up and grimaced. "I do believe I'm going to have a few bruises to show for this."

Handing her the cloth, Fiona slipped her arm around Mrs. Marcussen's shoulder and guided her to an upright position. "Lean against me, and I'll help you into your seat."

"All right." She took a deep breath. "I'm ready."

Moments later, breathing heavily and looking even paler, the widow hunched into herself on the chair, pressing the handkerchief to her laceration. She pointed a trembling finger at Fiona. "You've got a large bump on your forehead, dearie. How are you feeling?"

"A bit of a headache, but I'll be fi—"

The door slammed against the wall, and two men wearing bandannas over their noses and mouths clattered into the car. Wearing a black Stetson and long leather coat, the taller of the two waved a revolver. Significantly shorter, the other man carried a rifle and a canvas sack.

"Don't nobody move," Black Hat shouted. "This can go one of two ways." His voice rumbled deep in his chest. "You can put your money and jewels into the bag, and we'll be on our way, or you can try something funny and end up dead. Understood?"

Fiona's pulse pounded as she gaped at the thieves. Iowa was apparently more uncivilized than she expected if outlaws were able to rob trains at gunpoint. What was she getting herself into?

Chapter Two

Sweat trickled between Keegan O'Rourke's shoulder blades as he hammered the final nail into the wood frame. His muscles strained against his cotton shirt bringing to mind the times he'd scaled the ropes to the crow's nest. He missed the smell of the ocean, but it hadn't taken long to realize farming was just as difficult...and satisfying as sailing despite the challenges.

Too much sun was as dangerous for the crops as not enough to say nothing of the rain or the threat of insects, such as locusts. Working the land was a bit like Goldilocks—needing everything to be just right. He pulled out a handkerchief and mopped the perspiration off his forehead, then stepped back and surveyed the crew of men swarming over Seamus's property, like ants at a church picnic. A lightning strike had burned his friend's barn to the ground a week ago, and within two days the community had rallied to build a replacement.

A community similar to the one he'd fled in Ireland. Simple and hardworking, the people of Tullaghan would give away their last pair of pants to a neighbor in need. Not like the peerage who seemed more interested in finding success on the backs of their tenants and continued to persecute the Catholics just for having a different faith. Why couldn't they leave the Irish alone to do as they wished?

He blew out a sigh and stuffed the linen cloth into his pocket. He might miss the Old Country, but if he'd remained on the Emerald Isle, he would have ended up in a pine box like his brother Eoin, a bystander who'd been at the wrong place at the wrong time. The boy hadn't deserved to die, but the constant skirmishes between the powers that be and those who wanted to toss Mother England out of the country didn't discriminate between the innocent and the guilty.

His lips twisted, and his stomach hollowed. Yes, coming to America had been the best decision he'd ever made, but the choice had come at a cost. A steep cost. Would he ever see his parents again?

"Hey, boyo, are you here to work or supervise?"

Keegan turned as Seamus approached, a sloppy grin on his face and a glass of water in each hand. "Aren't you the clever one? I could ask you the same, except I'd be looking a gift horse in the mouth." He took the proffered drink and drank it dry. "'Tis early in the season to be such a scorcher. Doesn't bode well for the summer."

"Agreed." Seamus downed his water, then wiped his mouth with his sleeve. He clapped Keegan on the shoulder. "Thanks for helping with the raising. I owe you one."

"No, it's I who owe you for taking me under your wing, but we'll call it even now." He squinted at the hulking structure. "We should finish boarding her up by dinner, then we'll start on the roof tomorrow. She's a beauty, to be sure."

"That she is." Seamus peered at him. "Seems you've got something on your mind. You wouldn't be worrying about your young bride chugging her way to see you?"

With a shrug, Keegan dug the toe of his boot into the dirt. "Seemed like a good idea at the time, but what if she takes one look at me and the shack and realizes she's made the worst mistake of her life?"

"Nonsense. You're a fine, strapping lad that any woman would be pleased to have as a husband. And that so-called shack is a decent cabin. Let her look at some of the soddies around here, and she'll be proud to call your place home. I'll tell her myself just how much you've accomplished in the eighteen months you've been here. You proved your residency and purchased the title already. Granted, you've got four more years to stay and make additional improvements, but the time will pass quickly."

"I did have a good first season, even made a tiny bit of profit." He grinned. "I guess I'm all right."

"You're still stinging from life across the pond, with the gentry filling your ears with insults and innuendos. We Irish are as smart and able-bodied as anyone else, no matter what anyone says."

Keegan frowned. "The Old Country isn't the only place where we're mistreated. I heard enough coming across the country. We're on the bottom rung in the East as well. I heard about the signage saying No Irish Need Apply. If I'd stayed in the one of the cities, I'd have ended up in just as much trouble." He shook his head and forced a smile. "Bah, enough of that. We've got it good now. Des Moines has been gracious and open-armed."

The clang of iron against iron cut through their conversation.

Seamus tossed a glance over his shoulder. "Sounds like the ladies have lunch ready. I'm starving."

"Me too." Keegan cocked his head and jabbed his friend with his elbow. "Even if all I did was supervise."

A guffaw burst from Seamus's lips. "Right." He gestured toward the tables that were overflowing with platters and bowls of food, a feast that represented the various nationalities that made their way to Iowa from across the sea. Famine, persecution, and the chance of a new life had brought Scandinavians, and both Western, and Eastern Europeans to join those from the British Isles.

They sauntered to the tables with the other men. Children scampered and skipped across the yard while the women waited nearby. Seamus raised his hands, and silence fell over the group. "Dear Father God, thank You for providing these friends who are graciously giving of themselves and their resources to help Madeline and me. Who have drawn beside us during this difficult time. Thank You for the food we are about to eat. Bless the hands that prepared it. May we always recognize Your sovereignty in our lives. In the name of Your Son, Jesus, amen."

"Amen." Keegan opened his eyes, peace settling on his shoulders like a warm blanket. Seamus was right: God was in control. He had taken care of Keegan until now and would continue to do so. He didn't understand why his heavenly Father had allowed Eoin to be killed, but to let bitterness take root wouldn't solve anything. Unfortunately, choosing to lay down his hatred of the English and the Irish who supported them was a daily event...nay...sometimes hourly.

He picked up a plate and heaped it with boiled bacon and cabbage, Swedish meatballs, German potato salad, kielbasa, Croatian goulash, and a couple of items he didn't recognize but smelled delicious before making his way to the dessert table filled with cakes, pies, puddings, and pastries. How well did his new wife cook? Their letters had been stilted and brief, and she'd indicated she could prepare meals, but would they be palatable? Would he have the heart to tell her if they weren't?

"Stop worrying." Seamus jerked his head toward the porch where a line of chairs waited. "I see the crease between your eyebrows. Enjoy your food, and let tomorrow take care of itself."

"Wise words." Keegan climbed the steps, then nearly dropped his plate as a small child dashed out of the house and shoved his way past the two men. "Hey!"

Seamus chuckled. "Better get used to it. You'll have some of your own, and you can't let your wife do all the raising, especially if you have boys. They'll need a father's firm and loving hand. That'd be you."

Keegan gulped. "First, I'll settle for getting to know my wife, a good Irish lass. There's plenty of time to worry about children down the road." His heart stuttered. Was he ready to be a husband and father?

Chapter Three

Perspiration trickled down the sides of Keegan's face as another unseasonably hot day enveloped the train station. Shouts, laughter, and conversation mingled with the creak of wagons and trunks hitting the platform. Five minutes had elapsed since any passengers disembarked. His gaze ricocheted from face to face. No one seemed to be searching for him.

The pungent odor of coal clung to the air, and steam wafted above his head. A beefy, uniformed porter sauntered toward him, a smile on his wrinkled face. The man met his eyes and dipped his head in acknowledgement before walking past.

Keegan whirled and studied the man who stopped near a trio of women and gestured toward their luggage and then the station. Gray-haired and petite, the oldest of the three well-dressed women nodded. With practiced motions, the porter hefted their bags onto his shoulders and headed into the low-slung brick building. The clock in the tower struck noon.

Stuffing his hands into his pockets, Keegan gritted his teeth and turned back to the train. Nothing. No young woman scrambled from inside apologizing for her tardiness. No officials sought him out with a message.

Apparently, Miss Quigley had changed her mind and absconded with the train fare. Why would she do that after sending a telegram that she'd gone through with the proxy ceremony?

He blew out a deep breath and stomped toward the buckboard. Had he missed a clue in her letters that would have indicated instability or subterfuge? Worse, had he misread what he felt was God's leading to agree with Seamus's scheme of using a mail-order-bride agency to find him a wife? Should he contact his parents to see if any of their village lassies would be interested in a new life in America?

His face heated as he climbed into the wagon and dropped onto the hard wooden seat. He could only imagine the ribbing he was going to get when word leaked out that he'd been thrown over. No matter. He'd survived worse in the Old Country.

"Hyah." He clicked his teeth, then gave the horse's rump a gentle slap with the reins. The mare bobbed her head as she pulled the conveyance along the dusty thoroughfare. He'd wasted enough time for one day. There were plenty of chores to be done that would take his mind off the debacle of being robbed of both money and pride...and potential happiness.

Traces held loosely in his palms, he rested his elbows on his knees as the buckboard lurched and trundled toward his homestead. "Help me understand what happened, Lord. I'm angry, but if I'm honest, my pride's what's stingin'. It hurts to be rejected, and she didn't even have the decency to let me know herself. I thought she was the one for me. Her letters...she seemed to be a woman of faith...not perfect, but one of integrity. How could You let me be duped like that?"

The horse nickered as if in agreement, and Keegan's lips twisted. "Sorry, Father. This isn't Your fault. Help me figure out what to do. She took nearly all the funds I had, so I won't be able to pay for an annulment or another bride. Not that I'm ready to rush into *that* any time soon."

Within minutes, he'd left the hustle and bustle of town behind. A hawk swooped on the thermals high in the cloudless sky. From its zenith, the sun warmed his back. On either side of the rutted road, fields shimmered with yellowish-green seedlings that poked through the dark earth. Iowa might not be the Emerald Isle, but the state shone with a beauty of its own.

His shoulders sagged as the muscles unclenched. He shot a wry glance at the heavens. "Thanks for the reminder that You're in charge. You brought all of this into being with a few words. Surely, You're watchin' out for me."

The barn came into view, and he smiled. The sting of rejection still clawed at him, but with time the pain would dissipate. Meanwhile, God had blessed him with a fertile plot of land and good friends. As if she, too, was anxious to be home, the mare picked up her pace. His smile widened, and he gave the animal her head. Moments later, they rolled into the barn.

He jumped from the wagon and unhitched the mare. After hanging the tack on the wall, he brushed her from head to tail, murmuring as he worked. Once finished, he scooped a generous portion of oats into the trough to keep her busy while he mucked out the stall.

A loud sigh slipped out, and he chuckled as the tightness in his back eased. Amazing how a bit of manual labor always soothed his frantic thoughts. Nothing like good, honest tasks caring for animals lightened his load. He forked fresh hay into the enclosure.

At the sound of approaching hoofbeats he lifted his head, then leaned the tool against the wall and hurried to the doorway. Seamus hurtled toward him on the back of a huge bay stallion. The steed's heaving sides didn't bode well. His friend slid from the saddle as the magnificent horse came to a stop.

Heart pounding, Keegan rushed forward. "What's happened?"

Seamus yanked a small envelope from his back pocket and thrust it into his hand.

Fingers trembling, Keegan slit the flap and withdrew the telegram. His gaze raked the page absorbing the brief message. "Miss Quigley...er...Fiona never made her connection. The train was robbed, and she's at Mercy Hospital." He crumpled the missive and hurled it to the ground. "I'm such a fool. I've been upset thinking she changed her mind, and she's been injured this whole time."

Seamus clapped him on the shoulder. "You couldn't know."

"Perhaps not, but I let my temper get the best of me again. I jumped to conclusions. Am I ready to be a husband?"

Fiona scooted the chair closer to the hospital bed while the doctor examined the tow-headed, three-year-old girl. The child had also been injured during the robbery, but her parents fared much worse. Witnesses told about her father's bravery...or foolishness in trying to reason with the thieves. They'd shot him and his wife, then stripped them of money, jewels, and anything else they deemed of value. Now the little girl was an orphan, and Fiona had agreed to take her in.

She'd met the family early during the journey, and they'd grown close, with her watching Cassie to give the young couple some time alone. Eager to begin their new life in Iowa, they talked about the plans to develop their farm. Like Fiona, they'd also come from the city and wanted a fresh start with clean air and land that stretched for miles.

The doctor tousled the toddler's hair and smiled. "You're right as rain, little one, and ready to go home." He slipped the wooden tube that he'd called a stethoscope into his pocket. "Thank you for allowing us to keep her for observation. With one so young, she can't tell us how she feels, so it was best to keep an eye on her."

"I agree, and I thank you for your time." She nibbled her lower lip. "I...uh...don't have much money, but will pay what I can for her care."

He held up a hand. "No need. There was a well-to-do couple on the train who made arrangements for her fees."

"But the thieves—"

"Didn't get everything they came for." He winked. "The rich don't carry all their money on their person. Enough about those outlaws. With any luck, they'll be captured and brought to justice. Let me take a look at you."

She smoothed her bangs away from the tender skin of her forehead, and the doctor studied the bump on her forehead, then peered into her eyes. "You're also fine. Your pupils are the same size and respond to light correctly, so there doesn't seem to be an internal injury. The area will be sensitive for a few days and will be discolored for a while, but you should make a full recovery. If you don't see improvement within three days, contact your local doctor."

"Yes, sir." She rose and scooped Cassie in her arms.

The child wrapped her arms around Fiona's neck. "Mama?"

"Your mama's gone to be with Jesus, little one. I'm going to be your new family."

"Mama?" Tears welled in Cassie's eyes, then tumbled down her cheeks.

Fiona's heart clenched as she stroked the child's back. She exchanged a glance with the doctor over the toddler's head and sighed. She turned and strode from the dormitory-style room, her heels clacking against the wooden floor. What did she know about mothering? And what would Keegan say when he saw the child? In his letters, he'd been gracious and open, but that didn't mean he'd appreciate being blindsided by her decision to raise Cassie.

She froze at the doorway. Would he make her send Cassie to an orphanage? Her pulse stuttered. Surely not. She'd find out soon enough. He should have received her telegram by now and hopefully would be waiting at the Des Moines Station when she arrived tonight. She shifted the child on her hip and headed down the hallway. She entered the tiny room that served as a reception area.

Hats clenched in their fists, two travel-stained men hovered at the desk. Both stood a few inches under six feet. The beefier of the two had piercing, ice-blue eyes under a full head of strawberry-blond hair, its red highlights gleaming even in the dim room. His companion's hair was a nondescript blond. Both were tanned from hours in the sun.

The redhead's gaze shot to hers and then widened. Uncertainty danced across his features. "Miss Quigley...I mean Fiona?"

"Keegan?" Fiona clutched Cassie closer to her chest. "What are you doing here?"

"I received your telegram. I wanted to see how you were, and to bring you home so you didn't have to take the train."

"That's very kind of you." She frowned. This was not how she envisioned their first meeting.

The man with Keegan cleared his throat. "I'm Seamus Fitzpatrick. Would you like to get something to eat before we set off for Des Moines?"

Keegan blinked. "Yes, of course. Dining." He gestured to Cassie. "Who is this? Are her parents injured as well?"

Fiona licked her lips. The moment she dreaded arrived. How would he react? "This is Cassie. Her parents were killed during the robbery. I've agreed to raise her."

His lips thinned, and his face darkened. "Without thinking how I might feel about that?"

She gulped. There was no question how he felt about her decision, and the answer wasn't good.

Chapter Four

Cassie whimpered, and Fiona kissed her cheek. Did the child sense Keegan's acrimony toward her? Why was he being so difficult? Was it so terrible to take in an orphan? Was this an indication of his inability to care for others? Her palms moistened. Was she destined for a loveless marriage? Her head throbbed. Too many questions.

She lifted her chin and rolled her eyes toward the young woman behind the desk, who was watching them with keen interest. "I'd prefer not to discuss this in the middle of a hospital reception area. Is there somewhere we might go for privacy?"

His face reddened, and he clapped his Stetson onto his head. Blue eyes glittering, he gave her a curt nod and gestured toward the door. His friend murmured an apology and stepped back. At least one of them had manners.

Head held high, she swept past the two men and marched out the door. The heat slammed into her like an oven, and she squinted at the glare. If it was this hot in May, what would August bring? Would she be here in August?

"This way." Keegan jerked his head to the right, and she followed him to a large wagon parked under the trees.

A massive, reddish-brown horse with black ears, mane, and tail was tied to the back of the conveyance. Seamus untied the horse and swung into the saddle. He touched the brim of his hat. "You two have much to discuss, so I'll be on my way. It was a pleasure to meet you Miss...er...Mrs. O'Rourke."

"You as well, but let's not stand on ceremony. Please, call me Fiona."

He winked. "A good Irish name. I'd be happy to." His glance slid to Keegan. "Take all the time you need. I'll stop by the farm and take care of the animals."

"Thanks." Keegan nodded as Seamus turned and rode away. He watched him for a long moment, then cleared his throat. "Can I assume your baggage is at the station?"

"Yes, they were kind enough to store it for me." Her stomach growled, and her face flamed.

His face seemed to soften for an instant, then the steely gaze returned. "We'll grab something to eat at the diner, then retrieve your things before heading home. Let's save our discussion for the ride, if you don't mind."

"Of course." She set Cassie on the seat, then lifted her skirts and climbed into the wagon. Thrilled she hadn't fallen on her face in the effort, she pulled the toddler into her lap.

"You did that real well, but I'd have helped you." A glimmer of respect shone in his eyes. He trotted around the wagon and scrambled on board. With a flick of his wrist, he got the horse moving. The wood creaked as the vehicle lurched forward.

Aware of his proximity, Fiona tucked her elbows close and remained silent as he drove through town, making several turns before parking in front of a small building with a covered porch. Large windows flanked the bright-yellow front door. Pots overflowing with petunias lined the steps. The aroma of cooking meat mingled with the fragrance of herbs and spices. Her mouth watered, and her stomach rumbled again. She pressed her lips together and sighed. He'd think her graceless and gauche.

"I'll take the child so you can get down." Uncertainty flitted across his face, but he held out his hands. "I'm sorry I don't have a carriage."

"Nonsense. What use would a farmer have for a carriage?" She nuzzled Cassie's neck, then whispered, "You're going to be all right. Go to Kee—Mr. O'Rourke."

The child's eyes widened as she looked toward Keegan, but she reached for him without a sound.

Fiona let out her breath. At least Cassie hadn't screamed or cried. Neither of those behaviors would have endeared the child toward her new husband. She got out of the wagon, and he handed Cassie down before jumping to the ground. With the hand on the small of her back, he led her up the stairs and into the café. Her skin tingled with his touch.

An hour later, they'd eaten without incident, retrieved the trunks and satchels from the station, and were on their way to his farm. The meal she'd enjoyed now sat like lead in her stomach at the realization it was time to talk about Cassie, who had fallen asleep against Fiona's shoulder. At least the child wouldn't have to hear herself discussed...perhaps even argued about.

Perspiration trickled down Fiona's back adhering her dress to her back as the sun beat down on them. The slight breeze only served to push hot air onto her face. She'd lost her hat during the chaos of getting Cassie to the hospital and replacing it hadn't come to mind until now. She'd burn before asking him to return to town to the milliner's. And she'd also let him begin what promised to be a distasteful conversation.

Silence enveloped them for several miles. He glanced at her several times, then finally blew out a deep sigh. "We've much to discuss, and I know you must be weary, but it's best we get this over and done with."

"Agreed."

"I guess you can see I was a bit, uh, surprised at the sight of the child."

"Cassie."

"What?"

"Her name is Cassie."

"Of course. Anyway, why did you agree to take her? Didn't you ask the railroad about relatives? Surely, there's someone in the family who could take her."

"I did speak with the authorities, and they have no information about her parents. I got to know them over the course of the trip, and their parents are all dead. They made no mention of siblings or extended family." She narrowed her eyes. "Would you have had me take her to an orphanage?"

He shrugged. "Would that be so terrible? She'd be with other children her own age."

"You can't be serious. A child needs to be with a family, not with paid staff members. Haven't you read about these places? They're overcrowded, and few have enough money to properly care for the children. Many of them plunk the kids onto orphan trains and sell them to the highest bidder."

"Then they would be with the family you think is so important."

"Don't you?"

He tugged at his hat. "Yes, family is important. I just don't understand why you think we need to be her family. And why you were willing to make the decision without taking me into consideration."

Cassie snuffled in her sleep and wiggled in Fiona's arms, so she used the opportunity of settling the toddler to gather her thoughts. She straightened her spine and leveled her gaze at him. "I'm sorry for not including you, but speed was of the essence. I didn't have the luxury of waiting for your arrival. As I said, I did check with the authorities about the possibility of family, and after my conversations with Cassie's parents, I honestly don't believe there are relatives who could take her. Granted, I've only known her a few days, but to send her away to strangers wasn't acceptable to me. I plan to keep her, and if that is repugnant to you, I'm willing to go through whatever process is required to have our marriage annulled."

He reared back, his eyes wide. "Whoa. That's not necessary, but would you do me the favor of allowing me to pursue whether or not she is truly an orphan? I would hate to take the child from her biological family. That wouldn't be fair to her or them."

She nibbled her lower lip. Did he truly want what was best for Cassie, or did he not want to raise another man's child? Or is it children in general he didn't like?

Chapter Five

Keegan cast a sidelong glance at Fiona. The sun glistened off her ebony hair, reminiscent of a raven's wings. She was bent over the child, and the curve of her neck was as graceful as a swan's. Her blue eyes were averted, but he didn't need to see them to recall their cobalt-colored depths. They'd changed hue three times over the course of the day: pale and icy when they'd met, nearly turquoise when she looked at the little girl, and gray when she'd gotten feisty.

She'd had every right to be upset with him. He'd jumped down her throat minutes after meeting her. She'd survived a harrowing ordeal, lost newfound friends, and shown courage in the face of uncertainty, and then he'd barked at her for an act of kindness. He could have waited until after she was settled in his home to address her decision.

Forgive me, Lord. I've let my own uncertainties influence me. Guide me and help me to be a husband after Your own heart. I'm not sure I'm ready to be a father, so I'll need Your help if that's what You've got planned for us. He shook his head. An instant family. He'd barely gotten used to the idea of being married, and now he had a child to look after, too. God did have a sense of humor.

The wagon dipped into a rut, and Fiona was thrown against his side. The clean scent of her hair and another fragrance...lavender, perhaps...enfolded him. Her hand flew to his thigh to brace herself, and a jolt shot to his hip. She snatched back her hand, and his gaze shot to her face, red and blotchy.

He tightened his grip on the reins. His cheeks were hot, attesting to his own red face. "Sorry, must keep better attention on the road. Dolly knows the way home, so I let her have her way. Are you all right?"

"Yes. Just startled." She shrugged. "I've had little exposure to horses. Are they all as smart as she is?"

"Definitely. And sensitive. Horses are wonderful companion animals. Just as loyal as dogs. I also have chickens, a goat, and a cow. Once you get comfortable, you'll be responsible for collecting the eggs and milking the goat and cow. Over time we'll figure out what you know how to do and what Madeline—that's Seamus's wife—needs to teach you. I would imagine life is different in the city compared to the farm."

"Strikingly so." She gave him a wry smile. "For starters, I haven't seen any goats or cows."

Keegan chuckled. "Then I look forward to introducing you." He sobered. "Back to our conversation about Cassie. Do you agree to let me contact the railroads to see if she has any family?"

Her shoulders slumped as she nodded. "You're right. It wouldn't be fair to raise her if she had real family who could look after her." She ran her fingers through the child's silky, blonde hair. "I've already grown attached. It would be painful to lose her."

"We'll pray about the situation, but I understand. You're tenderhearted."

Fiona wrinkled her nose. "Which has gotten me into trouble over the years."

"Brought home a lot of strays, have you?"

She giggled, the sound carrying on the breeze like silver bells. "Wounded kittens and lost dogs. Even a squirrel, one time, but Mum put her foot down on that one."

"As well she should. They don't belong inside."

Cassie awakened and sat up. Blinking, she stretched out her arm and poked his shoulder, then yawned and rubbed her eyes.

He pressed his lips together. She was a cute one. He'd have to guard himself if he didn't want to lose his head over the child. She belonged with her family if she had one. "I've not been around small children, so I'm not going to be much help with her." A poor excuse, but the only one he had at the moment.

"I could teach you."

"You could."

"You sound skeptical." She smirked. "Or is that fear I hear in your voice?"

"Ha, never."

"Doggies?" Cassie pointed to a sheep-filled pasture. "Pwetty."

"Not dogs, little one. They're called sheep. Baaa!" He rolled his eyes. Great, now he was making animal noises.

"Baa," Cassie mimicked him, and Fiona beamed.

A fierce desire to protect the two of them swelled in his chest. Is this what it was like to be a husband?

"They're much bigger than I thought they would be. And there are so many of them."

"'Tis a massive industry in Iowa. We produce more sheep than any other state or territory. Some are used for food, but most are kept for their wool production. I've considered adding a herd, but need to get my feet under me with produce first. The state also has an enormous number of cows, so cheese is also a big industry."

"I had no idea." She studied the fluffy beasts as the wagon trundled past the field. "I think I'd like to know how to make wool, but not cheese."

"I'll keep that in mind when I'm expanding. You can even name all the sheep if you think you can keep them straight."

"You have big plans."

"I do. Farming is unlike anything I've ever done, and it's backbreaking work, but the satisfaction of a job well done at the end of the day is fulfilling."

"In your letters you told me about sailing. Do you miss it?"

"The ocean, yes, toiling for a hard taskmaster, no. I'd much rather work for myself." He gestured to the rolling hills. "The landscape undulates like the sea, and there are some small lakes in the area I'm able to visit, so I've adjusted. The area developed after Fort Des Moines was constructed to control the local tribes that were moved here from the eastern part of the state. Some folks wanted to name it Fort Racoon after the river, but the government put its foot down. Coal mining started nearly ten years ago, which is a mixed blessing."

"It's beautiful, and so open. I've lived in Boston my whole life." She shrugged. "Few trees to speak of except in the parks."

"You'll need to adjust being away from the ocean as well."

"I rarely went to the water." She lifted one shoulder in a half-hearted shrug. "No, what I'll miss is the aroma of corned beef and cabbage or colcannon as I walk down the street. Or the sound of children playing stickball in the street. 'Tis quiet here. I'm used to the cacophony in the city."

"The country makes noise." He winked. "But not at the volume you're used to. And we do have Irish, although the Germans may soon outnumber us. There are other Irish folks in the community, many of whom attend our church."

"I look forward to meeting them."

"Do you still have family in Ireland?"

"Probably, but my parents lost touch with the family when they left Armagh."

"Armagh? You're from Ulster?" A chill swept over him. "Are you Unionist?"

"What?" Confusion clouded her features. "I'm from Boston. You know that."

"But your family hails from the northern reaches." She'd failed to mention her heritage in her letters. Was the omission on purpose? He gritted his teeth. He'd been a fool not to investigate her background. And now he was hitched to a Unionist.

Chapter Six

Gray sunlight seeped through the curtains as Fiona rolled over in bed. She sat up and stretched, then unbraided her hair and ran her fingers through the long tresses. Her gaze went to the space beside her on the mattress. Keegan hadn't forced himself into the room to share her bed: a topic they hadn't discussed in their letters. The subject loomed large last night as the clock inched forward. When she could hardly keep her eyes open, he informed her that he would be sleeping in the barn.

Had that been his plan all along, or had the presence of Cassie complicated things? Still slumbering, the child lay bundled in blankets on a small, straw-filled pad on the floor, thumb tucked into her mouth. Was Keegan waiting until their feelings developed into the love two married people share, or was there another reason he didn't join her?

They'd gotten along well enough last night, but would he answer her truthfully if she asked him about his decision to bed in the barn? Her face warmed. Or would he see her question as an invitation? What if he rejected her? What if he didn't? She blew out a deep breath and swung her feet to the floor. With quiet motions, she washed her face with the tepid water in the pitcher, then changed from her nightgown into a dress. After brushing her hair, she pinned it into a bun at the base of her neck.

The smell of frying ham wafted into the room, and her mouth watered. She poked her feet into her shoes, then bent to wake Cassie. The child sat up, confusion wrinkling her brow. "Mama?"

"Mama's not here, sweet thing. Are you hungry?" Perhaps if she diverted Cassie's attention, she wouldn't miss her mother.

"I want Mama." The little girl's chin trembled. She knuckled her eyes, then let out a wail. "Mama!"

Fiona's heart clenched as she drew Cassie into an embrace and stroked her hair. "I know you do, but your mama and papa are with Jesus now."

The door swung open, and Keegan stood on the threshold, his face a mixture of confusion, irritation, and concern. "What's wrong with her?"

With a finger to her lips, she shook her head. As Cassie's cries abated, Fiona mouthed, "She wants her mother."

His expression softened, and he nodded. "Take all the time you need. I'll keep breakfast warm."

"I seem to have overslept. I'm sorry I didn't rise early enough to cook."

"Not on your first morning. But I'll expect that to change tomorrow." He gave her a mock frown. "Besides, you'll want to handle the meals after you've eaten mine."

Fiona snickered, the tension slipping from her shoulders. Perhaps this marriage would work out after all. Moments later, she'd managed to quiet and dress the little girl. Thumb stuck between her lips again, Cassie toddled beside her out of the bedroom.

Keegan jumped up from the table and pulled their food from the oven. He set down their plates filled with fried ham slices and scrambled eggs, then poured two glasses of water. "I don't know what little girls eat."

"The same as we do, just not as much." She helped Cassie onto the chair, then dropped into the one next to it.

"Okay." He poured two cups of coffee and placed one in front of her.

She inhaled the fragrant brew. He claimed he couldn't cook, but his coffee smelled divine. She handed Cassie a spoon, then cut the child's meat into bite-sized portions. She waited until Cassie began to eat, then nibbled at her food. Keegan was right about his abilities in the kitchen. The eggs were dry and crumbly, the ham scorched in several places.

The silence stretched. Times like this made her aware of her lack of social graces. Finishing school had not been in the cards. After Da's death, her mother had taken in laundry for a short time before coming into her own as a seamstress. Then Fiona had followed in her footsteps. They were sought after for their skills with a needle, not for brilliant conversation.

"I...ah...don't know what your plans are for the day, but I will need to go to town to obtain fabric so I can make clothes for Cassie. I have a few things in the satchel that came with her, but I didn't think about searching for her trunk."

He rose and lifted the lid on a chest by the wall. The smell of cedar floated in the air. "Madeline told me a wife would appreciate such things, so there is a variety of material in here as well as the...uh, notions, I believe she called them."

Fiona clapped her hands. "She's right. This is a treasure trove." Satisfied that Cassie was intent on her plate, Fiona joined Keegan and plunged her hands into the sea of fabric. "Such a beautiful selection. Did you..."

"Oh, no. This is all Madeline." He smiled. "I'm pleased it makes you happy."

"Very. And after I finish with the garments, I can use my skills to add to the family coffers."

"What?"

"I told you in my letters I'm a seamstress. My fancy work was in demand in Boston. I can help earn money. I mean...I would get all my chores done first, but..."

His eyes narrowed, and his lips thinned to a slash. "Do you think I can't provide for you? I may not be rich, but we will have enough."

"That's not it. I have skills. Why not use them to our benefit?"

He climbed to his feet. "You'll have enough to keep you busy, and I don't need you to earn money." He marched to the door. "I'll be in the barn. When you're finished, I thought we could tour the farm, familiarize you with the land. The trip to town can wait."

"Wait! We need to discuss this." Her heart hammered in her chest. "I'm sorry for offending you, but please stay." Fiona held out her hands. How could he take offense at her offer? She hadn't intimated he couldn't provide for her. How could he get so upset at her suggestion? She loved sewing, especially adding embellishments to an outfit. Why not use a task she adored to help support the family?

Were all men this sensitive, or was Keegan alone in being easily insulted?

"Why would you think I can't provide for us?" His hand on the knob, Keegan spoke through wooden lips, "I thought I made it clear in my letters that even though I've only been here a little over a year, the farm is doing well, and I'm earning my way." He rubbed the back of his neck, then crossed his arms. "First, you decide to bring a child into the marriage without so much as a by-your-leave, and now you're undermining me by suggesting we need the income. Are you going to back me into situations for the rest of our lives?"

Sapphire eyes blazing, she straightened her spine, seeming taller than her diminutive five-foot height. "We've already discussed Cassie, and I admitted the decision was hasty and thoughtless; however, I was not ready to leave the orphan on her own even if you are. As far as undermining you? That was not my intent, and I meant no offense. I have been taking care of my mother." Her voice broke, and she swallowed. "I had to provide for her as she sickened, but in doing so I found joy in my work. Creating attire for women that makes them feel pretty and perhaps better about themselves brings me happiness. It would mean a lot if I could continue to do so."

Keegan's shoulders sagged. He'd done it again. Let his pride get in the way, reacting in anger. His lips twisted in a wry smile. But she'd given as good as she got. And the tongue-lashing was well deserved.

"Please, let's sit down and discuss our marriage." She spoke in soft tones, the same he'd use with a skittish colt. "Cassie can play with her doll while we talk. Unless you need to get to your chores."

"I took care of things before you rose. There's plenty of time." He cleared the table, then waited behind her chair as she wiped Cassie's mouth with a damp cloth, then picked her up and set her on the floor. She giggled as Fiona danced the doll across her lap, then into the child's arms.

Patting her hair, Fiona sat, and he scooted her chair forward, inhaling the scent of lavender that floated toward him. He lowered himself on the chair next to her. "I apologize for making assumptions and getting angry. Please forgive me."

"'Tis forgotten. I'd hazard a guess that we're both a bit nervous about this whole proposition." She sent him a dazzling smile, and a dimple appeared on her left cheek. "My parents were partners in love and in life, and I hope that we can be the same." Her face pinked, and she ducked her head. "Not right away, of course, but someday. What are your mum and da like?"

Visions of his parents appeared in his mind, and his throat thickened. He swallowed past the lump.

Fiona patted his hand, then laced her fingers in her lap. "You miss them very much, don't you?"

"More than I thought I would. I took them for granted when I lived close by, and now I'm not sure I'll ever see them again."

"We'll write them often. Perhaps that will ease your pain."

"A wonderful idea, and they can get to know their new daughter." He licked his lips, looking at Fiona in a new light. Despite being hurt by his words, she tried to soothe his troubles with kind words and actions. "They're good people, hardworking. He is a fisherman, and she keeps the house, but also does a lot of work with the church. Visiting shut-ins and taking food to the poor...that sort of thing."

"They sound lovely. I look forward to getting acquainted."

"Listen, how about you get settled in here for a month or so, getting the hang of juggling your chores with caring for Cassie and making her clothes, then we will talk again to see if you feel you have the time to add being a seamstress. Does that sound fair?"

"Yes." She nibbled her lower lip and fiddled with her skirts. "Cassie may not be here in a month if you find relatives who want to take her."

"We'll—"

Cassie howled, her eyes screwed shut, and her mouth wide open.

Fiona jumped up and rushed to the little girl, then gathered her into a tight embrace.

Keegan narrowed his eyes. What in the world had caused the child to cry, no, not cry, wail, like a banshee? So much for finishing their conversation. Would it always be like this? The wants and needs of the child coming before his own?

Chapter Seven

Rain thrummed on the roof overhead as Fiona opened her eyes and yawned. The second morning of her new life had begun. Careful not to wake the slumbering child, she crawled from the bed and donned her clothes in the darkness. She and Keegan had come to an uneasy truce. Why was his first response to flee when they disagreed? Her parents had followed the biblical adage not to let the sun go down on their anger, so on more than a few occasions she heard their voices late into the night as they tried to resolve their differences.

He'd given her a tour of the farm, much larger than she'd expected. Although he'd been on the property little more than a year, he'd built a barn in addition to the tiny cabin and cultivated every inch of land. She could see the pride on his face as he pointed out the boundaries and talked of his future plans. He'd been patient and kind when he'd shown her how to milk the goat and two cows, and collect the eggs.

Her muscles ached from her shoulders to her fingertips, and her skin was tender from where the chickens pecked her for stealing their eggs. She'd better toughen up, or she wouldn't be able to hold a fry pan or cook pot.

Another yawn overtook her. She'd fallen asleep as soon as her head hit the pillow. How could she be so tired? She shuffled out of the room with a sigh. Yes, she'd better toughen up, or Keegan might send her back to Boston.

She tiptoed to the kitchen area and grappled for the matches on the table. She lit the lamp, the acrid smell of sulphur filling her nose. With a twist, she adjusted the wick until a soft glow pushed back the shadows of the room. She lit the stove so that it would heat while she collected the eggs and pumped water.

Her gaze fell on a basket filled with eggs sitting on the counter. She blew out a sigh. Had she overslept again, and Keegan performed her chores? Her fingers wrapped around the white orbs. Still warm.

"I couldn't sleep."

Nearly jumping out of her shoes, she turned. Her pulse skittered, and she pressed a hand against her chest.

Hair in disarray, Keegan rose from the couch. "I'm sorry. I didn't mean to startle you." He went to the door and propped his rifle against the wall, then walked toward her. "The coyotes were active last night. I thought it best to keep watch over you and the...uh...Cassie."

"But what about the animals?" Her voice sounded breathless in her ears.

"The barn is snug, but I went outside periodically. Hopefully, my human scent deterred the beasts' desire to come close."

"You must be chilled to the bone. I'll start the coffee."

He shrugged. "The rain didn't start until about an hour ago, but I wouldn't mind a cup or two."

Aware of his proximity, Fiona poured water and grounds into the coffeepot, then set it on the burner to boil. She grabbed two mugs from the shelf. Her hands trembled as she set them down, and she gave herself a mental slap for her schoolgirl reaction. How could she be affected by his presence after only forty-eight hours? What would she be like at the end of the week?

His flannel shirt strained against the muscles in his back as he reached for plates, then he stretched around her to put them on the counter. The mixture of leather, perspiration, and a unique scent she'd come to associate with him filled her senses, and she closed her eyes, fighting the desire to inhale. She needed to get a grip or she'd be useless.

She glanced at the pail of milk on the floor next to the stove and lifted one eyebrow. "Did you do all my chores this morning?"

"I told you I couldn't sleep."

"How did the girls feel about being milked before sunup?"

He chuckled and rocked on his heels. "Not happy."

"Breakfast won't be long, but if you've been awake all night, you might want to take a snooze on the couch until it's ready."

"No thanks." Keegan nudged her shoulder, then crowded close. "I think I'll help you."

"I thought you said you couldn't cook." Tilting her head, she looked up at the man towering over her. Goodness, he was tall. "H-how can you help?"

"Got you flustered, eh? My plan is working." His voice was smooth, like warm syrup. "You can teach me your secrets. Because my pancakes are either too dry or get crispy edges, and I hate that."

"All right." She took a deep breath and jabbed him with her elbow. "But you need to give me some space."

Keegan yelped, then laughed and moved away. "Yes, ma'am."

A giggle escaped, and she scooped flour into a bowl. "Much better." Was it? His closeness had made her more nervous than a cat in a room full of rocking chairs, but now she felt bereft of his presence. Their letters had been friendly and warm, but he'd made no declaration of love when he suggested they were suited to marry. Would he ever feel anything for her?

Rubbing the spot where she poked him, Keegan grinned. His new bride was an enigma. Alternately shy and sassy, she had a depth he hadn't expected. Her intelligence had come through during their correspondence but not her wit or fiery temper, when pushed against her convictions. A mixed blessing, to be sure.

He hadn't counted on her beauty either. They'd agreed not to exchange photographs, claiming compatibility and shared faith were more important than looks. At the time he'd wondered if she concurred because of being unattractive. That was hardly the case.

Her ebony hair gleamed, and her blue eyes were the color of a summer sky, sparkling or glittering dependent upon her mood. His fingers itched to stroke her cheek to discover if its porcelain creaminess was as soft as it appeared. He considered his own looks average at best. Was she disappointed with what she saw?

"Keegan?"

"Huh? Uh, sorry." His face was warm, and he rolled his eyes. Did she realize he was mooning over her? "Just woolgathering."

She sent him a saucy smile. "And how are you going to learn if you don't pay attention?"

"I guess I won't." He shrugged. "Start again, and I promise to hang on your every word."

"All right. First, you want to whip the eggs and add the milk to them before pouring the mixture into the flour. You'll get fluffier pancakes that way." She handed him a fork and gestured to the eggs. "The best way to learn is by doing."

He saluted, then took the fork, their fingers grazing. His skin seemed to sizzle where she'd touched him, and he nearly dropped the utensil. If he didn't stop his clumsiness, she'd think him an oaf. If she didn't already.

With awkward motions, he stirred the eggs.

"No. Like this." She cupped her hand over his to show him the correct movement. "See?"

Intent on the bowl, her head was cocked close to his chin. Close enough for him to place a kiss on the top of her head. Where did that come from? He cleared his throat. "Yes, I get it now."

"Good. Keep going until they're frothy."

With a nod, he continued to work.

Fiona peeked into the bowl, then added some milk. "Perfect. Now, combine these two and pour the mixture into the flour when you think it's ready."

"Confident I can figure that out?"

"No, but one learns by trial and error."

He guffawed, and her face pinked, which made him laugh harder. Yes, she was a delightful combination of shy and sassy. And he wanted her approval. Even for this simple task. He eyeballed the egg-milk mixture, then dumped it into the flour which sent a cloud of dust into the air and over the side of the bowl. "Oops."

She squealed and jumped back. "Gently, Keegan! You're not busting broncos."

"This is harder than that."

"Just different." She lifted one eyebrow. "Or are you trying to do such a bad job, so I'll never ask you to cook?"

"I wish it were so. Apparently, I'm naturally clumsy when it comes to the kitchen." He shrugged and blended the ingredients. He felt like an idiot, yet was having the time of his life. "How's that?"

"Well done." A smile bloomed on her face. "We're ready to cook them." She gestured to the iron skillet. "The secret is to put just enough lard in the pan to keep them from sticking."

"And how do I know that?"

"More of that trial and error." She poured three dollops of batter into the skillet. "You want to keep an eye on the edges. When they look a little dry, it's time to flip the cakes." She handed him the spatula.

"Me?" His eyes widened. "Busting broncos is easier than this."

She beamed, and her laughter filled the kitchen.

His chest swelled. How was it that he felt like a hero by bringing a smile to her face, even if it meant making a fool of himself? This was nothing like spending time with Seamus. He loved the man like a brother, and they'd spent many hours in camaraderie, but he didn't seek to make his friend smile. No other woman affected him like this, and after only two days. What was happening?

His brother's image swam into his mind's eye. A victim of the troubles with the mother country. Dead because the British thought they had a right to lord their presence over the Irish. Was he being disloyal to his principles with his marriage to Fiona? She was Irish, but she wasn't. Coming from the Ulster region made her English, didn't it? His heart was warring with his head. Who would win?

Chapter Eight

Creaking and groaning, the wagon lumbered down the hard-packed road. Keegan held the reins lightly in his gloved hands. The scorching heat of the last few days had been replaced with cooler temperatures, and a light breeze stroked his face. Late-afternoon sunlight cast long shadows in front of the buckboard as they headed to Seamus's homestead.

Beside him, Fiona sat ramrod straight with Cassie in her arms. Thumb stuck between her lips, the child studied him with a piercing gaze. How could such a little girl be so serious? Did she know she was an orphan? She hadn't cried for her mother since yesterday, but her drooping shoulders and wrinkled brow attested to her sense of loss, even if she didn't yet understand it.

They'd settled into a routine, and Fiona was already getting the hang of juggling the many tasks associated with running a farm. She was up before dawn to complete her chores in the barn, then in the kitchen by daylight to prepare a delicious and filling breakfast. He hadn't realized how bad his cooking was until he partook of her meals. She provided simple fare, but his mouth watered just thinking about the pot roast he'd devoured last night. He rarely ate vegetables, but he had two servings and considered a third the previous evening.

Then he found himself offering to help with the dishes. She'd turned him down, instead asking him to read aloud to her while she worked. He'd been embarrassed to admit he didn't own any books, but she'd assured him the Bible had plenty of exciting stories. In the flickering firelight with Cassie lying on the couch nearby, he regaled her with the tale of Jonah and the whale. She'd finished the washing in no time, then drawn the child into her lap, running her fingers through the little girl's cornsilk-colored hair. The homey ambience wasn't lost on him and brought to mind the tiny cottage in Ireland.

He nudged her shoulder. "You've done well in the short time you've been here. You should be proud of all you've learned." He patted his stomach. "And I'm grateful for the skills you bring to the kitchen."

As anticipated, her face pinked, and she shrugged. "Cooking is the easy part. 'Tis dodging the chickens' beaks when I'm swiping their eggs and milking that are proving to be a challenge. The poor cow looks quite indignant during the entire process. Fortunately, the cows seem more resigned to being subjected to my clumsy attempts."

"They've already been through my own heavy-handedness. There are few cows on a ship, so I had no practice."

Her mouth twisted in a cheeky grin. "Well, I'm not totally without talent. After all, I've had to wrangle difficult society women. Perhaps that prepared me more than I realized."

Keegan chuckled. "I'm imagining a lasso around their fancy hats."

She snorted a laugh, then covered her mouth with one hand, her eyes twinkling.

They rode in silence for several minutes, and he reveled in the feeling of companionship. He cleared his throat. "What was it like to live in the city?"

"Cramped. Dirty. Dangerous." Her eyes took on a distant stare. "But it was home, and we had lots of friends. We were in it together. Scraping to make ends meet and find enough to eat. Much like the early church, we shared among ourselves. After Da passed, they surrounded Mum and me, helping us find our way. Then when Mum got ill, they took turns staying with her so I could work." A single tear slipped down her cheek. "Despite the hardship, I miss them. Not that I'm unhappy here...I didn't mean to—"

He patted her knee, then drew back as if burned. Too intimate a gesture after only four days. "O-of course you're homesick. It's to be expected. Honestly, I miss the Old Country at times. Our village also gave of its dearth. Selfishness had no place there."

Concern continued to cling to her face. "What can you tell me about Seamus and Madeline?"

"You have much in common. She married Seamus by proxy." He snapped his fingers. "She's also from Boston and lost her parents as well. She'd been her father's caregiver for many years, long enough that she had no prospects for a husband. When her da passed, he left the house to a cousin who turned out to be as crooked as a dog's leg."

"How awful for her."

"But it worked out in the end. The cousin got what was coming to him, and she is happily married to my good friend." He snickered. "By all accounts, Seamus wasn't sure how it was going to work out. Madeline's mother died when she was young, and the servants handled the household chores. She could barely cook when she arrived."

"No wonder you're relieved at my capabilities in the kitchen." She cocked her head. "Would my lack of cooking skills have been a deal breaker? Would you have put me on the next train back to Boston?"

He rubbed his chin in mock consideration. "Hmm. Difficult questions, to be sure."

Fiona swatted him, her laughter filling the air. "Be careful how you answer."

"Or you'll do something diabolical with my food?"

"That would be too obvious."

"Ha! Apparently, I'd best keep an eye on you."

She lifted one shoulder in a delicate shrug, her eyes dancing. Cassie roused, and Fiona bent her head toward the child and whispered in her ear.

Keegan's heart tripped. Their posture was reminiscent of a painting he'd seen years ago of *Madonna and Child*. The same love streaming from her eyes. The same protective curl of her arm around the little one. Could he grow to love Cassie as Fiona seemed to? Could he raise another man's child as his own?

Chapter Nine

Pulse skittering, Fiona handed Cassie to Keegan, then climbed from the wagon. She retrieved the toddler, cradling her close. The little girl could walk, but carrying her would give Fiona something to do. After working with countless clients, she should be used to meeting new people, but it never got easier. Feelings of inadequacy washed over her.

Would his friends like her? Her breath caught in her throat, and her mouth dried. She shifted Cassie onto her hip and straightened her spine.

The door swung open, and a slender woman about her own age and perhaps seven or eight inches taller, hurried onto the porch. Her auburn hair was pulled back on either side of her face with combs and tumbled down her back. Snapping brown eyes shimmered as she drew Keegan into a quick embrace. She then turned to Fiona and squeezed her shoulder. "You must be Fiona, but who is this little one? She's beautiful."

Cassie squirmed and ducked her head. Fiona lifted her chin with a gentle finger. "This is Cassie. She lost her parents on the train ride to Des Moines. Smile for Mrs. Fitzpatrick, sweetie. She's our friend."

Madeline's face fell. "How sad. Then it is a blessing she has you, isn't it?" She gestured toward the house. "Let's go inside where we can be more comfortable. I can't wait to hear all about you."

"I hope you're hungry. She made enough to feed a dozen people." The look he shared with his wife brimmed with love and pride. He clapped Keegan on the back. "Your new bride is lovely, old man. How'd you manage that?"

"Mind your manners, Seamus." Madeline poked her husband's chest. "She doesn't know you yet."

Face warm, Fiona forced a smile and followed Keegan into the house. Larger than it looked from the outside, the cabin was tidy and inviting. The walls were whitewashed and reflected the glow from the lamps that had been strategically placed around the room. Gauzy white curtains hung at the windows, and a multicolored quilt covered one wall. A fire danced in the hearth.

Snuffling sounded, and her gaze shot to the cradle near a rocking chair. "You have a baby." She hugged Cassie. "See the baby, Cassie? You used to be that tiny."

Madeline beamed. "She's two months old and already a daddy's girl. He spoils her rotten."

"She deserves nothing less." Seamus puffed out his chest and rocked on his heels. "Come, let's eat before the food gets cold." He gestured to chairs on the far side of the table. "Fiona, you and Keegan are over there."

An hour later, they'd eaten their fill and were lingering over coffee. Dinner had been a scrumptious selection of Irish dishes taking Fiona back to her childhood. Memories of her mother puttering in the kitchen swept over her, and her chest tightened. She blinked. When would the sharp stabbing pain from Mum's death dull?

Seamus wiped his mouth with a napkin, then pushed back his chair and stood. "If you'll excuse us, Keegan and I will see to the barn chores." He stroked his wife's cheek. "You outdid yourself tonight, Maddie."

Madeline gave him a dismissive wave. "And you've been kissing the Blarney stone again."

"Nonsense." He winked. "Well, no more than usual."

She giggled. "Get on with you."

Fiona swallowed a sigh. Would she and Keegan ever get to a place of loving teasing?

The men clomped out of the house, and Madeline climbed to her feet. "How about we ladies chitchat while we do the dishes? Unless you're all talked out."

"Not at all." Fiona rose and carried Cassie to the couch where she curled up against a cushion. "I was nervous to meet you, but you and Seamus are so warm, I feel right at home. I'm glad to have a new friend. I...uh...don't make them easily."

"How are you settling in? It's only been a few days. You must feel a bit unsteady on your feet."

"Somewhat, but Keegan has been patient with me. The chores with the animals are a little disconcerting. Not the goats so much, but the cows are huge." She wrinkled her nose. "And stinky."

Madeline chortled. "Yes, that's what I had to get used to. The city has its own smells, but they are familiar. The animals are...earthy."

"He works hard, and he's already made some changes or additions to the house to make things easier for me."

"I'm not surprised. Under his bluff and blather, he's a good man. He'll do right by you." She cocked her head. "And he seems to be quite taken with you, even after only a few days. That bodes well for the future of your marriage."

Fiona's cheeks warmed. "He was upset when I showed up with Cassie. He said I should have included him in the decision."

"He's still very much of the Old Country sometimes. He'll come around." Madeline jerked her head toward the little girl who chatted with her rag doll. "You did a good thing taking her in. Most orphanages in this country are barbaric."

"We may not get to keep her. He's contacting the Pinkerton Agency for them to search for relatives. I'm trying not to get attached, but it's difficult."

"She is a darling." Madeline pumped water into the sink, then added hot water from a pot on the stove. "I'm no theologian, but I find it hard to believe God would bring her into your lives only to take her away.

After all, He brought you and Keegan together. Why would he create a family, then tear it apart?"

Fiona barked a dry laugh. "I stopped trying to figure out God's plans a long time ago. I would appreciate your prayers. I'm praying too. Harder than I've ever done, but I won't force Keegan to raise her."

"Then we'll have to pray God changes his heart."

"Or mine."

Keegan grabbed a scoop and dug into the barrel of oats while Seamus fed the chickens. They worked in silence for several minutes.

Setting down the bucket of corn kernels, Seamus walked to the wall of farm implements and selected a pitchfork. He leaned on the handle. "I like your new bride. A bit shy, perhaps, but that's to be expected. How are you getting along?"

"Well enough." Keegan shrugged. "As you know, we exchanged letters, and I felt I knew her through our correspondence. But the real thing? Apparently, the letters only scratched the surface. She's got a mind of her own."

Seamus chuckled. "Not as malleable as you thought? You want a partner, Keegan, not a puppet."

"I know, and neither of us is used to seeking the opinion of others before acting, but it's made for some interesting situations."

"Like finding yourself with a child."

"Exactly." He rolled a nearby cart to the stall so Seamus could fork the soiled straw into the conveyance. "I'm barely prepared to be a husband, let alone a father."

"I've got news...you'll never feel ready. Maddie and I'd been married over a year before the baby was born, and we're still trying to figure things out. But one thing is for certain. We love that child with all our hearts and will stop at nothing to ensure she's protected and provided for."

"But Cassie is another man's child."

Seamus raised his eyebrow. "And that man is dead. Now, I'm not saying I fully understand what you're feeling, but that little girl needs you to be her da. Unreservedly. If you can't do that, you should find her another home. She needs to know you fully love her."

A deep sigh escaped, and Keegan wheeled the cart outside to dump the contents and give himself time to respond. Purple and pink streaks of the setting sun stretched across the sky. Pinpricks of light twinkled, and a slight breeze ruffled his hair. God reminding him of His presence? Keegan returned to the barn. "I've contacted the Pinkertons to find her family."

"A wise decision. She deserves to be with her own." Seamus tossed the last of the bedding into the cart. "But what if there is no one to take her?"

"She'll remain with us." Keegan swept the remaining dust and debris out of the enclosure. "I've already committed to that with Fiona."

"There are plenty of folks in the church who can help you. Lord knows, Maddie and I have availed ourselves of lots of advice over the last two months. It's not a weakness to ask for help." His lips twisted as he began to distribute clean straw on the floor. "I've had to learn that the hard way."

"Fiona seems to know what she's doing as far as caring for the child...bathing, feeding, disciplining. That's not the issue."

"No. It's the constant interruptions at the inopportune times."

"Exactly!" Keegan's breath exploded in a loud sigh. "Every time Fiona and I sit down to have a serious conversation, the child cries or needs to be fed or go to the outhouse or simply wants attention. It's maddening."

"And exhausting." Seamus hung up the pitchfork. "But it is the most rewarding thing you will ever do. Think about it, old man; you're shaping the life of another human being. Being an example of our heavenly Father. There's nothing else you will do that is as important."

"You're supposed to be encouraging me. Now, I'm more terrified than when I arrived."

Seamus guffawed and clapped him on the back. "Then I know you're up to the task. Because that's how I feel every day."

"But how will Fiona and I get acquainted if we're constantly barraged by Cassie's needs?"

"'Twill be a challenge. I won't lie, but that's where Maddie and I, and your other friends from church come in. We'll take care of her, giving you a reprieve and time together. Pastor Upton and his wife have done that twice thus far for us. With Aidan being so young, we can't be gone long, but even an hour without responsibilities is a relief." He crossed his arms. "You're not alone, Keegan. You've got a community behind you, but more importantly, as a believer, you've got your faith to sustain you. Pray about the situation...that if God chooses to have you raise this little girl as your own, that He'll help you find the love in your heart for her."

Keegan tugged at his ear. What did the future hold? And how soon would he have the answer?

Chapter Ten

Fiona fingered the tissue-paper pages of her Bible as she listened to the pastor's words. On one side, Cassie leaned against her, fiddling with the ruffle on the dress Fiona had finished the night before. On the other, Keegan sat seemingly riveted on the sermon. With good cause. Pastor Upton's rumbling voice was gentle yet insistent as he spoke about God's plans. He'd used Jeremiah 29:11—her favorite verse—as the basis for his sermon, then went on to share story after story of examples in his life and that of people from the Bible to prove his point.

She glanced around the room that acted as the town's schoolhouse during the week. The benches upon which the small congregation gathered were plain but sturdy. A scarred table stood front and center, presumably for the teacher. The bookcase held a collection of worn McGuffey Readers. Memories of learning to read with her own copy of the textbook assailed her. Would she have the opportunity to teach Cassie how to read using the much-loved book?

"Beloved, I understand that it is difficult to wait upon the Lord. Even when we know in our hearts that whatever He has in store for us is for our best and for His glory. We often run ahead of Him, forging our path and then beckoning for Him to follow. When things don't work out, we're surprised or stunned. We think 'How could that happen?' But if we're honest with ourselves, we know the answer."

The preacher grinned, dimples forming on either side of his mouth, making him look impish. "Many of you are aware of my history before coming to serve as your leader. I was the pastor of a large church. Hundreds belonged to my flock. We had buckets of money, and many of my members were powerful, influential people. I was sure I had *arrived*."

He shook his head. "I had heard God's call to serve in rural America, but I was sure I knew better. I thought if I served a bigger congregation, I would be doing more for the Lord. A bit like Jonah, I was running from God's plan and miserable for it. Fortunately, because of my wife's wise counsel, I stand before you now as your pastor. Unlike me, she was listening to His words." He fell silent and gazed at the dark-haired woman located on the front bench, flanked by two identical-looking, six- or seven-year-old boys. Love poured from his eyes that shimmered with unshed tears.

Fiona gaped. She'd never seen a man exhibit such emotions. Wasn't he afraid the church would think him weak? Da had never shed any tears. Even when her mother lost her little brother days after he'd been born. Perhaps her father cried behind closed doors, alone, but she doubted it. He exuded strength from morning until night. The day he left for war, he'd stood straight and tall in his uniform, embraced Mum, then stroked

Fiona's cheek. Marching beside her uncle, he'd turned and saluted before disappearing around the corner.

Was Da's death part of God's plans? Her heart thudded in her chest. No. Da died because men couldn't agree that slavery was bad or whether states had a right to choose. The country had split over the argument, finally going to war. Too old to be drafted, her father had signed up to prove his love of his new country. She'd overheard him talking to Mum who tried to convince him that he didn't need to go. But he'd told her about his bosses. How they said the Irish weren't real Americans. He said a man had to stand up for his convictions.

Had Da listened to God when he decided to go to war? Or had he run ahead like the pastor talked about? Either way, he'd been killed, leaving Mum and her to fend for themselves.

But all had worked out. Life had been difficult, but the two of them had done all right. Finding joy in their sewing and being able to provide for themselves. They'd learned how to keep a ledger and calculate the expenses in order to know how much to charge for their work. Maybe Da's death wasn't part of God's plan, but He definitely guided Mum's steps, and then hers. He'd arranged Fiona's marriage, so she was taken care of after Mum's death, but was He responsible for her being nearby to take care of Cassie, or was that simply a coincidence? She rubbed her forehead. Too many questions.

The congregation rose and began to sing "Amazing Grace." Her face heated. She'd been so caught up in her thoughts that she missed the end of the sermon. But she'd heard enough to realize that no matter what happened, God was in control. She would trust Him and do her best to follow Keegan's lead rather than running ahead on her own. Even if it meant losing Cassie.

Keegan rose and held out his arm. She tucked her hand in the crook of his elbow, then held out her other hand to Cassie. The child slipped off the bench and toddled along behind them as they wended their way to the door. Madeline and Seamus waved from across the room, and Fiona dipped her head in acknowledgment. Her first Sunday, and the tiny congregation already felt like home. "I liked what Pastor Upton had to say. Are his sermons always so practical?"

"Yes. I learn something new every week. He's a kind and humble man, typically using himself in his illustrations, much like he did this morning."

She shuddered. "I don't think I could be as forthcoming about myself."

"Agreed. I've no hankering to share my faults with a room full of people." He winked. "One person is more than enough."

A giggle escaped, and warmth like a blanket settled on her shoulders. Stepping outside into the sunshine, she squinted against the glare. The sky was dotted with cotton-ball clouds, casting shadows on the mountains. "I don't think I'll ever tire of the majesty of the Rockies. I didn't realize what I was missing in Boston."

"They are something to behold."

"You know she's telling everyone the child's parents were killed during a train robbery." A strident voice cut the air. "Does she really expect us to believe that?"

"There was an incident last week. I read about it in the paper."

"How convenient." The voice dripped with sarcasm. "No, the child is hers, and she made up the story to cover her shame. I'm sure of it."

"I heard Keegan didn't know about the little girl until the woman arrived."

Fiona gasped, and tears sprang to her eyes. So much for feeling like a family. Apparently, society women in Boston weren't the only ones to indulge in idle gossip. She glanced at Keegan to see if he'd heard. His darkened face told her he had. His mouth thinned to a slash, and he released her arm.

"Remain here." He strode to the two women who were oblivious to his approach as they continued to titter and speculate about Fiona. He stopped in front of them and cleared his throat.

They turned as one, and their eyes bulged at his appearance. Faces pink, they had the decency to look ashamed. The taller of the two said, "Mr. Keegan...uh...how are you today?"

"Disappointed that you think standing outside the church disparaging my wife is acceptable behavior." His eyes glinted. "You know nothing of what you speak, and saying it loud enough for all to hear is unconscionable. Fiona is no liar. Perhaps the sin in your own life causes you to seek sin in others so you'll feel better about yourselves."

The women's mouths opened and shut like the fish Fiona had seen gasping for breath in the nets at the harbor.

Keegan's brow came together. "You owe her an apology. Immediately. And if I hear that you've continued spreading these falsehoods, I'll have you brought before the congregation. And when you get home, you might consider reading the first chapter of James and the fourth chapter of Ephesians."

They hurried past him to Fiona, mumbled an apology, then scurried away. Not the most heartfelt attempt at making amends she'd experienced, but Keegan standing up for her was what mattered. He hadn't hesitated to assure them of her integrity. As an Irishman, he might not like the comparison to Sir Lancelot, but he'd been her knight in shining armor.

Chapter Eleven

While Cassie played on a blanket near the couch, Fiona finished preparing her contributions to the barn-raising luncheon at Seamus's house. After much consideration, she'd settled on making potato salad— one of her favorite childhood dishes—sugar cookies, and corn bread. Madeline had only asked for a side dish, but in her agitation over last Sunday's incident, Fiona cooked and cooked. And cooked.

A wry smile played on her lips. It had always been that way. Whenever she was upset, she'd find herself in the kitchen making enough food for an army. Then Mum would come in and press her to talk, and the words and tears would come tumbling out.

"Oh, Mum. I miss you so much." Her eyes welled, and she blinked away the moisture. "What would you have me do about the women?" She wrapped the pan of warm bread in a towel, then began to plate the cookies.

Cassie chortled and murmured to her rag doll.

Fiona glanced over her shoulder at the little girl, who'd finally stopped asking for her parents. Had she already forgotten them? Would the town take that as proof she wasn't an orphan but rather Fiona's illegitimate offspring? How would they treat the child? With pity or disdain?

Had the people who would be at the barn raising today heard the gossip? Did they think her a liar and a fallen woman? Would they shun her?

Her stomach clenched, and she pressed her hand against her middle. Maybe she and Cassie should stay home. She could send the food with Keegan.

"What do you think I should do, little one?" She straightened her spine. "Since when am I a shrinking violet? I've handled arrogant society matrons and nitpicky customers." She sighed. "But they didn't cast aspersions on my character. They didn't spread untruths about me."

"Do you really think she's going to give you an answer?" Keegan stood in the doorway, arms tucked into his front pockets and a playful grin on his lips.

She'd been so intent on the situation, she failed to hear the door open. Her face heated, and she shrugged. "Sometimes it helps to think out loud."

He strode across the room and grasped her arms, turning her toward him.

Trembling, she focused her gaze on his chest. She didn't dare look into his face, letting him see what his touch did to her.

With a gentle finger, he raised her chin until she was forced to meet his crystal-green eyes. Soft, they were filled with care and concern.

"I heard what you said, but those old biddies treated you unjustly. You've got no cause for shame."

"But people may believe them, and then where will we be?" She swallowed the lump that had formed in her throat. "You've worked hard to build your life here. Your reputation. And in the span of ten days, I've besmirched your name."

"Hardly." He dropped his hands but remained close. "I learned long ago that people are going to believe what they want. They will seek out others whose thoughts align with theirs, no matter how many times they are contradicted. Therefore, we will go, and we will look them in the eye as if nothing is wrong."

"But—"

"Because nothing is wrong. We know the truth, and God knows the truth, and He will allow it to come out. Remember what Solomon said in the Proverbs: 'If your enemy is hungry, give him food to eat, and if he is thirsty, give him water to drink. For in doing so, you will heap burning coals on his head.' Easier said than done."

She heaved a sigh and nodded. "'Twill be easier with you by my side." She tried to smile, but her lips faltered. "Thank you for being such a godly man, and for defending me. You've believed me from the very start. That means a lot, more than you'll ever know."

He winked. "If you knew what was going on in my head, you might not think me so virtuous. I won't tell you what I'd rather we did to those women." He reached forward as if to stroke her face, then dropped her hand as his cheeks heated. "There is no reason for me not to believe you."

The clock on the mantle struck.

"We best be getting on." He seemed to search her face. "Are you feeling better about going?"

"Yes, although I can't say I'm excited about the prospect at this point."

"Understood." He picked up the towel-wrapped bread. "I can go to the pastor if you'd like. We've handled it thus far among ourselves, but I can get him involved."

"No. That would only cause worse feelings. Let us try to be kind to them."

"You're a good woman, Fiona."

She shook her head and mimicked him, "If you knew what was going on in my head, you'd not think me so virtuous."

Keegan roared with laughter. Her cheeks were tinged with a light shade of rose, and a smile tugged at the edges of her mouth as she picked up the dish filled with fragrant potato salad. She continued to surprise him with her quick wit. Life with his new bride would not be dull.

He lifted the platter of cookies and tucked the bread under his other arm. "Wait here while I hitch Dolly to the wagon, then I'll help you with the rest of the food and Cassie."

"Thank you." She put down the bowl, then went to the door and opened it for him.

Balancing the food, he left the cabin and headed to the barn. The sun warmed his back as he walked across the expanse between the two buildings. He began to whistle "All Things Bright and Beautiful," then grinned. Since when did he whistle?

As he entered the crude wooden structure, the mare poked her head over the stall wall and whinnied. He placed the food in the back of the buckboard, then sauntered to the enclosure.

"You fancy a trip, girl?" He stroked her muzzle, and she nosed his hand. He scratched the side of her face. "Shame on me. I forgot a treat for you."

She nickered and rolled her eyes.

He chuckled. "You're no longer the only woman in my life. I'm going to have to learn how to juggle the three of you."

With practiced motions, he grabbed the tack, led her to the wagon, and slipped the bit between her teeth, murmuring to her while he worked.

"Today's not the day, girl, but we need to teach Fiona how to drive. She's already making a difference inside the house." He frowned. "And despite being hurt by two busybodies, she's willing to forgive. I didn't know the church had such cruel people. They've all been welcoming to me, without a judgmental word to be had."

He picked up the harness. "Or did I not hear them talking behind my back?" He sighed. "She's done an honorable thing by accepting responsibility for the child. I wasn't happy about it when they arrived, and I'm still not sure how I feel, but I never doubted for a minute she lied about Cassie's identity. How can people make such awful assumptions about a person they've never met? Is society so rigid that good deeds get punished?"

Finished with putting the tack on the horse, he backed up the mare and connected her straps to the buckboard's tongue. "Let's go, girl." He led Dolly into the yard. "I admire Fiona, you know. She's not tattlin' to the preacher about what happened. She's willing to handle this on her own and try to let bygones be bygones."

"Do you always talk to her?" Laughter colored Fiona's voice.

He whirled, his feet creating a dust cloud. Great. His new bride must think him a total eejit. "She's a good conversationalist."

She cocked her head and squinted at him in mock censure. "Should I be jealous?"

"I'll let you know."

Her eyes widened, then she snickered. "If you'd like some time alone—"

"Perhaps later." He played along with her antics. "Now, daylight's burning, woman. Get in the wagon."

After an exaggerated salute, she took Cassie's hand, and they toddled to the buckboard. Fiona placed the food in the back of the wagon. A cheeky grin lit her face as she nodded toward the little girl. "I'll climb in, then you can hand her up to me."

Keegan glanced at the child as Fiona bunched her skirts into her hand and stepped onto the wheel hub and into the buckboard. Cassie no longer shied away from him or hid behind Fiona when he was close. She was getting used to him. What would happen if the Pinkerton agent found her family? Would she adjust to new people in her life? So many changes for one so young.

He took a deep breath and lifted her into the conveyance. Her tiny body weighed almost nothing, and a protective surge swept over him. Is this what it felt like to be a father? To realize that he would do whatever necessary to keep her safe? He glanced at Fiona, who beamed at him. His chest swelled. He could get used to making her smile.

Chapter Twelve

As the wagon rolled onto the lane that led to Seamus and Madeline's house, Fiona blew out a deep breath and wiped her damp palms on her skirt. She'd put on a brave face when Keegan asked her if she wanted to tell the pastor about the women who'd gossiped about her, but in reality her stomach roiled at the thought of seeing them again. Would they be more inclined to talk about her after Keegan's reprimand? Their apology certainly hadn't been heartfelt. Rather, they seemed embarrassed at getting caught.

He squeezed her hand. "You have nothing to be ashamed of, and Cassie is blessed to have you as her surrogate mother."

Her skin tingled where he'd touched her, and she pressed her lips against the gasp that threatened. How could he affect her so strongly after only ten days? She squared her shoulders and nodded. "Thank you."

The buckboard rattled and bumped over the rutted path. Voices and the sound of hammering floated toward them as they approached. Men darted in and out of the massive barn, carrying wood of various shapes and sizes.

"Should we have come over sooner?" Fiona watched the activities. "It seems they've already started."

"I told Seamus we'd be late. He has plenty of help, and I had some tasks that needed to be done today."

"Things I should have been doing?" She fidgeted on the seat. Was he still performing chores that were hers?

"No. I had a couple of repairs to make in the barn, and I've been putting them off. Once the growing season starts in earnest, I won't be able to get to them." He parked the wagon near the others and set the brake, then jumped down. He reached for Cassie and set her on her feet next to him. Fiona clambered to the ground, and her heel caught on her skirt. She fell against him, and his arms went around her. The clean scent of soap assailed his nostrils.

"Sorry. So clumsy of me." Her cheeks blazed. "Not exactly the entrance I wanted to make."

"I thought you wanted a hug." He released her and held up his hands.

Her jaw dropped. A moment later, she realized he was teasing and giggled. Once again, he'd tried to ease her discomfort. What a gracious man. "There will be no confusion when I'm looking for an embrace," she shot back, then clapped a hand over her mouth. She wouldn't have thought it possible, but her cheeks burned even hotter.

Keegan snorted a laugh and reached into the back of the wagon for the bread and cookies. "I look forward to it." One eyelid lowered in a lazy wink, then he turned and sauntered toward the food tables.

Heart pounding in her chest, she retrieved the potato salad, took Cassie's hand, and followed him.

Children raced back and forth in the meadow behind the house, their laughter and shouts ringing out. The women were scattered. Some supervised the toddlers, while others sat in the shade stitching a quilt. A few hovered near the food tables. Fiona's gaze ricocheted from face to face. She nearly stumbled in relief. The women who'd insulted her weren't in attendance.

Having left Fiona's contribution on the table, Keegan was deep in conversation with Seamus and a man she didn't recognize. Seamus pointed toward the doorway of the barn, and the trio ambled inside.

With a final look at the spot where the men had stood, she turned and walked to the quilters, Cassie's hand clasped in hers. Would they let her help or was it a closed circle? She nibbled her lower lip and fiddled with the strings on her bonnet.

A gray-haired woman in a faded floral dress tucked her needle into the fabric and stood. "You must be Mrs. O'Rourke. I'm so pleased to make your acquaintance. I was under the weather on Sunday and unable to come to services. My name is Bertha. What a precious child."

Fiona smiled at the woman's prattle. "Thank you. She is sweet."

"I know. I heard what you did, taking her in after her parents were killed in that awful train robbery. A tragedy, to be sure. I hope they catch those varmints. Do you like to sew? I'd love for you to join us."

"I've never quilted before, but I'd like to try if you think I won't mess it up."

"Nonsense. Quilting is easy as pie, but I also heard you're a seamstress, so you'll do just fine."

"You—"

"Yep. Heard all about you. Those old telegraph machines have got nothing on us ladies." The woman chortled. "Does Cassie need to stay close, or do you want Mabel here to take her to play with the rest of the little ones?"

Fiona squatted in front of Cassie whose neck swiveled like a top as she watched the hustle and bustle. "Do you want to go meet the other children?"

Cassie nodded vigorously, and the blonde woman Bertha had indicated rose and held out her hand to the little girl. "You can take my place. We'll have a grand time. Won't we, Cassie?"

The child waved at Fiona and skipped toward the field without a backward glance. And without her thumb tucked into her mouth. Perhaps Cassie was finally settling in. Now, if she could only do the same.

Bertha gestured to each of women around the quilt. "Inga, Greta, Winnie, and Nell."

"Thank you for including me. 'Tis a beautiful quilt. I'm not familiar with the design. What's it called?"

"This is a double-bear-claw pattern and one of my favorites. Keeping the points straight can be tricky, but I enjoy the challenge."

Sitting down in the vacated chair, Fiona picked up the needle dangling from the thread where Mabel had left it. Her fingers curled around the steel, and she sighed. How she loved to sew. Would she master running the household well enough for Keegan to allow her to ply her trade? Time would tell.

Conversation ebbed and flowed, and time passed quickly. Fiona's cheeks ached from smiling and laughing as the women engulfed her in friendship. Tears prickled the backs of her eyes. Mum would have loved these ladies.

Her stomach rumbled, and she pressed a hand against her middle.

"Sounds like it's time take a break for lunch." Bertha grinned and snipped the end of the thread, then pushed her needle into a small, round cushion.

The other ladies set aside their work and climbed to their feet. Fiona excused herself and hurried toward the field where Cassie raced after a little girl, a wide smile on her face. She caught sight of Fiona and wheeled toward her. She arrived at the fence red-faced and breathless. "I like it here."

Fiona laughed. "I do, too, little one. I do, too. Are you ready for lunch?"

Crawling under the crosspiece, Cassie nodded. "I hungry."

"Let's go find Keegan."

As they hurried toward the barn, the clanging of the iron triangle called the men to lunch. Fiona scanned the area for Keegan's familiar wiry form. She entered the building, the coolness of the dim space bringing relief from the midday sun. The drone of lowered voices came from the far corner. She peered into the shadows. Keegan and a man from church whose name she'd forgotten huddled closed together.

"I told you this needs to be done sooner rather than later. And keep it to yourself for now."

"I'll take care of it." The man turned, froze for a moment, then strode past her with a nod of acknowledgment.

Keegan seemed startled to see her. His gaze shifted to the ground, then he smiled and gestured toward the door. "I heard the bell. I'm ravenous. Did you have a good time with the ladies?"

She studied his face. What had he been discussing? Was he involved in something underhanded? Illegal? Had she married a common criminal? Should she leave and get an annulment before their relationship went too far? Then what? There was no reason to return to Boston, but perhaps she could earn a living in Des Moines or one of the cities. With little money in her pockets, her choices were few.

"Uh...yes. They're lovely."

"Excellent." He crooked his elbow. "May I escort you to lunch, ma'am?"

Slipping her hand into the bend of his arm, she nodded. He claimed to be a believer, yet was he involved in something dishonest? *Dear God, what should I do?*

A Bride for Keegan

Chapter Thirteen

Applause and shouts of congratulations filled the air. Keegan nudged Seamus, who waved his arm and grinned. Madeline stood next to her husband, tears shimmering in her eyes. The last board had been nailed into place rendering the barn complete. Shadows lengthened as the sun headed for the horizon.

Keegan rotated his shoulders to ease the stiffness. He'd be sore tomorrow, but the ache was worth it. Seamus had done so much for him when he'd arrived with a satchel on his back and hope in his heart. He'd have built the structure singlehandedly if needed. His friend deserved nothing less.

Seamus held up his hands, and the group quieted. He laced his fingers with Madeline's. "Friends." His voice broke, and he cleared his throat. "Friends, I know it is our community's way to help one another from small things to large, but Madeline and I want you to know how grateful we are. We don't take it for granted that you've set aside your own needs for a time to help us. We love each of you and appreciate your kindness. Now, the time for work is over. Let the festivities begin!"

More shouts and laughter, and the crowd broke up. A trio of fiddlers clustered under a copse of trees, their tune loud and lively. Several couples began to dance. Across the way, Fiona held Cassie on her hip, swaying to the music. Both wore joyful smiles. At some point, she'd expect him to join her for a song.

He sighed. A dancer he was not. He could never seem to match the movement of his feet with the rhythm of the notes. He'd trounced on more than a few girls' toes. Good thing he wasn't an English lord who spent evening after evening in the ballroom.

His pulse stuttered. Perhaps Fiona had. She'd be highly disappointed once she saw his fumbling attempts. Keegan ducked his head and strode to the fence where a handful of men played a game of rings. He was taking the coward's way out, but this was more to his liking.

A warm breeze lifted his hair and dried the perspiration trickling between his shoulder blades. He crossed his arms and watched the friendly competition between the players as they ribbed each other. With narrowed eyes, he studied the men. Quite a few were Irish, some old enough to have left the Emerald Isle during the potato famine, while others like himself fled the clutching fingers of the English whose grasp seemed to get tighter by the day.

About the same time as the famine, the Germans crossed the sea to escape political unrest that resulted in riots and rebellion, finally culminating in a revolution. He'd heard the Scandinavians were running out of room and saw America as a place to spread out. Since his arrival, the city saw a wave of Eastern and Southern Europeans who were willing to work in the coal mines. He shuddered. Mining was a dirty, dangerous job—one he couldn't imagine having to work.

The afternoon waned, and the iron triangle clanged, signaling that dinner was ready. He rubbed the back of his neck. He'd managed to avoid dancing until now, but surely Fiona would expect at least one turn around the floor after they ate. He trudged toward the food tables, then berated himself for his unwillingness. A *ceilidh* was about fun, not how well one could execute a reel.

Filling a plate, he surveyed the area and caught sight of Fiona and Cassie sitting on the porch, their legs dangling over the edge. He licked his dry lips and hurried toward them. "Have you enjoyed your afternoon?"

Fiona's face lit up, and Cassie wiggled her fingers at him. "It's been lovely. I'm so glad I came. You seem to have had a good time. Did you win any of the games?"

"One, but barely." He cocked his head. "You were watching?"

"For a bit. My da used to play rings. He was quite good...able to catch the hook from long distances."

"A pro, he? Listen, I...uh...owe you a dance...or two." Keegan picked at the food on his plate. "You can choose which ones."

She shrugged, her expression closed. What happened? One minute she seemed glad to see him, the next guarded. He gave himself a mental slap. Had she sensed his reticence about dancing and felt rejected? What a *bodhar*.

"I would very much like to dance with you, but...frankly, I'm quite bad at it. Two left feet, as they say. I've damaged more than a few young ladies' toes."

"Perhaps later." She took the spoon from Cassie, who'd been fiddling with the food on her plate, scooped up some cabbage, and held it in front of the child's lips. Like a small bird, she stretched her neck and opened her mouth. Fiona smiled and handed her the utensil. "You're a big girl. You can feed yourself."

Cassie nodded, her pudgy cheeks bulging as she chewed. The sun glinted off her white-blonde hair, and her eyes sparkled. She seemed to have adjusted to the loss of her parents. Or was she too young to understand? Either way, she'd taken to Fiona, following her around the house and falling asleep in her lap. He'd been stunned to see her running and tumbling with the other children.

He drained his water. "Do you need more to drink?"

"Yes, thank you." She gave him her cup and Cassie's. "We could both use some."

"Coming right up." He set his plate on the step and rose. Ambling to the table, he refilled their cups.

Seamus jogged toward him. "Fiona seems to be fitting in with the ladies. I saw her at the quilting circle."

"Yes, she said they'd been warm and welcoming. A nice change after the incident on Sunday with a couple of the ladies."

"What happened?" Seamus's eyebrows shot up. "Does Madeline know about it?"

"We've kept it to ourselves, but Fiona was hesitant to come today because she overheard two women speculating that she was lying about Cassie's parentage. That the child is actually hers in less than proper circumstances."

Seamus's face darkened. "That's terrible. Who is it? Are they here?"

"I'd rather not say at this point, and they didn't come today. I spoke to them, and they made a token apology." Keegan raked his fingers through his hair. "But how many others are wondering the same thing? Fiona's had it hard enough. She's making a new start, and having her reputation tarnished with untruths isn't fair."

"I'm glad you were there so you could handle it for her." He tapped his chin with his index finger. "I must say you were looking right cozy over there with her and Cassie. Might you be growing accustomed to your new family?"

"Looks can be deceiving."

"It's been less than two weeks. Give it time."

Keegan stuffed his hands into his pockets and hunched his shoulders. "How much time? Will I ever get comfortable? Getting to know a new bride is hard enough, but now I have an instant family. One I didn't ask for."

Seamus winced when his gaze slid past him.

A chill swept over Keegan, and he turned. Fiona stood behind him, face white and chin trembling. She'd obviously overheard him.

"We came to get our water." She spoke through wooden lips. "I'm sorry we're an inconvenience for you."

"I didn't say that." He reached for her, and she recoiled.

"Not in so many words." She bent down and picked up Cassie, her motions stilted. "Seamus, I believe I'm ready to leave. Would you be kind enough to drive us to the Gateway Hotel?"

"What? No." Keegan rubbed his forehead. "You're overreacting."

She avoided his eyes and shifted away from him. "Seamus?"

"You really should stay and discuss this, Fiona. Keegan is a good man. He may not be the best at making sudden adjustments, but he means well."

"I'll check with Madeline. Unless, of course, you won't let her take the wagon."

Seamus held up his hands as if in surrender. "I've got a compromise. How about if you stay with us tonight? You can each consider the situation on your own, but I'll expect you to discuss this *in full* tomorrow after church."

"That's acceptable." She gave him a curt nod, then her gaze flicked to Keegan before she turned on her heel and strode toward the house.

"I've done it now, haven't I, Seamus?"

"That you have."

Chapter Fourteen

The wooden bench dug into the back of Fiona's legs as she shifted for the umpteenth time during Pastor Upton's sermon. She stifled a yawn and glanced at Keegan out of the corner of her eye. He appeared as exhausted as she was. After a protracted conversation with Madeline during which she agreed not let her temper get the best of her yet again, she spent the night tossing and turning. Alternately praying for guidance and rehearsing what she wanted to say today, she barely slept. Grit coated her eyes, and she blinked to ease their burn.

She'd nodded at Keegan outside the church when she'd arrived, but they'd yet to speak. Her pulse raced, and moisture sprang to her palms in anticipation of the conversation. He had every right to be angry with her. His words had hurt her, but he was being honest about how he felt. Sharing his burden with a friend. And she'd faulted him for his emotions. The first thing she'd do was ask his forgiveness.

Would he accept her apology? Or had he realized they were unsuited? His gaze was shuttered. What emotions was he hiding?

She shifted again, and he cast a sidelong glance in her direction. Her chest tightened. He must think her no better behaved than Cassie. Or less so. She clenched her hands in her lap. Why did Pastor Upton have to choose the topic of marriage today? Or had God chosen it for him?

The man's points had pierced her heart, reminding her that she'd committed to Keegan, and that God expected married couples to stay together in all but the most extreme situations, none of which applied to the two of them. Although wed by proxy, the marriage was valid in God's eyes, and it was up to her to be willing to make the relationship work.

Maybe Keegan would never love her as a husband should, and maybe Cassie would find her family, but God guided Fiona's path to Des Moines, and she needed to stay the course. She'd allowed her prayer life to fall by the wayside in her struggle to figure out how to be a farmer's wife and caregiver for a small child, when she should have doubled her efforts in that regard.

Forgive me, Lord.

Tension slipped from her shoulders, and she sighed, this time with contentment. She peeked at Keegan to find him staring at her. She smiled, and the guarded expression dropped from his eyes. He returned her look, albeit somewhat tentatively.

The pastor intoned the benediction, and the congregation rose. Before Keegan could stand, she leaned over and whispered, "I'm so sorry for my actions yesterday. I let my mouth run away with my face again."

He chuckled, and his eyes lit up. "I'm sorry, too. The house is too empty without you. Will you come home?"

"I'd like nothing better."

"We'll take Cassie with us, so you can have time alone." Madeline looped her arm through Keegan's and winked at Fiona.

"That won't be necessary." He shook his head. "We need to learn how manage the interruptions."

"All right, but if you change your mind, feel free to bring her over." She leveled her gaze at them. "I'll be praying for the two of you."

"That kind of help I'll take." He gave them both a sheepish grin, his green eyes twinkling.

Fiona nodded, her cheeks warm. "Me, too."

"We'll see you soon." Madeline released Keegan's arm and wiggled her fingers in a departing wave as she edged her way into the aisle.

He bent and picked up Cassie. "Ready?"

She tried not to gape at him, her heart thundering. Had he decided to accept the little girl as his own, or was he simply being helpful? Apparently, she wasn't the only one God had been working on.

They made their way out of the building, shook the pastor's hand, and settled onto the buckboard. Cassie sat between them, her legs dangling over the edge of the seat. Fiona put her arm around the little girl's shoulder to prevent her tumbling into the back.

"Thank—"

"I—"

Keegan chuckled. "Normally, the polite thing would be to let you go first, but I want to apologize again for what I said."

"You were talking with a friend. Trying to figure out how to deal with an unexpected turn of events. You weren't directing your comments to me. I had no right to get upset." She licked her lips. "And as difficult as it may be to hear, I'd like you to be honest with me about how you feel...about Cassie and about me. I listened to the sermon today. You're the head of the household. It is up to you to make the decisions that are right for our family."

"Seems you've given this a lot of thought." He let go of the reins and gave her hand a quick squeeze. "And didn't get any more sleep than I did."

"Hardly any." She blew out a breath. "Cassie won't be the only one who needs a nap."

"Sounds like a great way to spend a lazy Sunday afternoon." He cleared his throat. "I want us to be partners. I liked what you said about your da and mum, and I see how Madeline and Seamus are. They talk and pray about everything, and don't make any decisions without being of one mind. And...uh..." He squirmed, blotches of red forming on his neck. "I'll continue to sleep in the barn until such time as we both agree I'm welcome in the bedroom. I do want this to be a real marriage, but I won't rush you or force you into anything."

"All right." The heat on her cheeks told her she was as red as him. She'd never had such a candid conversation with a man. Would it get easier as they got to know each other?

The wagon rattled down the drive that led to the house. His hands tightened on the traces. "You said you wanted honesty. We need to talk about your association with the Old Country."

Her breath hitched. "What association? I was born in America."

"To parents from Ulster."

Her forehead wrinkled. "Yes, but what does that have to do with me?"

"Why did your parents come here?"

"To escape the famine, like thousands of others who were dying." She cocked her head. "Why did you leave Ireland?"

"To keep from getting killed." His lips thinned. "It was only a matter of time."

Her eyes bulged, and her mouth worked as she tried to think of something, anything, to say. She finally blurted, "What did you do?"

"A bit of protesting. Some vandalism. Nothing too serious."

"How would that get you killed?"

"Because I was doing it to the Brits. I wanted them gone. Eire should be one, united together without others taking up space on our land, setting laws that clearly show how little they think of us. Laws that line their pockets and keep us from earning a decent living."

"I-I didn't know it was so bad."

"Your folks never spoke of it? The riots? The heavy-handedness of the leadership?"

"Not that I could hear. Maybe Da and Mum talked, but not to me." Tears sprang to her eyes. "He worked hard at being accepted as an American. That's why he enlisted. He wanted to prove himself. Prove his love of his new country. He was too old to fight, but he went anyway." Her voice broke. "And he didn't come home."

"I'm sorry for that. The war took too many good men."

"So think what you will of my roots, but I'm as Irish as you. I'm also American. I hope you'll accept me for me alone. Not for my heritage. Not for my ideology, but as a woman who came west for a fresh start."

Chapter Fifteen

Rain thrummed on the roof and pounded the ground outside the cabin. Fiona shivered and tossed another log into the fire. Despite being early June, the weather was reminiscent of spring in Massachusetts: cold and dismal. Trapped inside, she'd cleaned the house top to bottom, made three loaves of bread, baked a batch of cookies, and churned butter. Her shoulders ached, but satisfaction of all she'd accomplished made the discomfort bearable. Would that it were true Mum could see her being a proper farmer's wife.

Her heart tugged. Her mother's death no longer cut like a knife, but that didn't make the loss any less keen. A week had passed since she and Keegan had ironed out their differences, and some days were better than others, but there were too many occasions when she could use Mum's wisdom. How had she and Da made marriage look so easy? The reality of it was far from effortless.

On the one hand, she appreciated Keegan's strength of character, but on the other, sometimes the trait seemed more like stubbornness. He had very specific ideas on how things should be done, but as Madeline said, he didn't take to change, which made for some interesting conversations. What did he think of her?

He seemed to enjoy her company, his eyes lighting up when he saw her. A smile tugged at her mouth. And he teased her regularly, roaring with laughter the more uncomfortable he could make her. She hadn't thought herself naïve, but she'd fallen prey to several pranks and tall tales.

Cassie dozed on the couch, her rag doll tucked under her arm. Three nights ago, Keegan had started keeping her company when she put the little girl to bed. He'd taken over telling the bedtime story, then would kneel beside Cassie with his hands folded as she said her prayers. He'd make a big deal about getting up, which never failed to elicit a giggle from the child.

Rather than laughter, the sight of his muscles straining against his cotton shirt as he rose set Fiona's pulse to racing. Lastly, he'd stroke Cassie's cheek, then bend and kiss her head. What would it feel like to have him do that to her? She fanned her face. The room was suddenly too warm.

The door opened with a bang, and Keegan clomped into the house, shaking the wetness from his coat. "A gully washer out there." He shed his jacket, removed his hat, and hung them on a hook. His eyes sparkled even in the dimness of the cabin. "Someone's been busy. This place is shipshape." He rubbed his stomach, and his gaze shot to the kitchen table. "And you made cookies. Bless you." He grinned as he strode across the room and grabbed three.

Tongue-tied, she nodded and wiped her hands on her skirt. He wasn't a large man, but his presence filled the house like a bull moose.

"No sign of the weather abating, and I've finished all the repairs in the barn." He winked. "Thought I'd see what you ladies were up to."

Sitting up, Cassie yawned, her mouth forming a perfect O.

"Well, one of us was napping."

To his credit, his face flamed. "Uh, sorry for waking her."

"No matter. 'Tis nearly time for lunch. But your penance is entertaining her while I finish putting the meal together."

"Fair enough." He finger-combed his hair, then went to the couch and scooped Cassie into his arms. "How about a dance, little one?" He executed a waltz, whirling in a wide circle.

Cassie chortled, and her face shone.

Tears pricked the backs of her eyes. Memories of dancing with Da consumed her, and her chin trembled. Why did the vision of Keegan embracing Cassie bring sadness? Would she ever stop missing her parents? The dip and rise of her emotions today was making her dizzy. She took a deep breath. The savory aroma of the pot roast filled her nose.

Lunch! She'd gotten so caught up in her emotions, she'd forgotten about the meal. Good thing the cookies were already done. They'd be scorched for sure. She grabbed two towels, opened the oven, and pulled out the roast. Her stomach rumbled as she carried the pan to the table. She added the basket of corn bread, then poured three glasses of milk. "All right, you two. Lunch is served."

"Excellent!" Keegan danced Cassie to the sink. "Must wash up."

Fiona watched as he made a game of soaping their hands, then rinsing them under the pump and drying them. He was more jovial than usual. What had happened in the barn?

Crossing her arms, she waited as he made his way to the table. "Suddenly you can dance? What happened to two left feet?"

"Are you jealous?" He grinned and gestured at Cassie's feet, then indicated the distance to the floor. "The secret to success is to keep your partner's feet out of reach. I can't trod on her toes because they're at my waist."

She slapped her forehead. "Of course! Why didn't I think of that?" She sent him a wicked smile. "At the next social, I'll expect to dance accordingly."

Keegan threw back his head and laughed. He tucked Cassie onto a chair than wagged his finger at Fiona. "Be careful what you ask for."

The air crackled between them, and she hurried to her seat. What had she been thinking to make such a brazen comment? Good thing he thought she was being clever rather than wanton.

After saying the blessing, he forked a potato chunk into his mouth. Closing his eyes, he moaned. "You've outdone yourself. I'd say this is better than my mum's."

"Do you have a piece of the Blarney stone hiding in the barn?"

"I'll never tell."

They ate in companionable silence, and Cassie managed to feed herself without incident or whining. She must be hungry, tired or both. A small blessing.

He mopped the last of the gravy with his corn bread and popped the bite into his mouth. "A meal fit for a king." He fiddled with his napkin and cleared his throat. "I...uh...wanted to let you know, I'm willing to adopt Cassie if no relatives can be found to take her."

Fiona's pulse stuttered. One step closer to being a family. Was it wrong to pray that no one would come forward?

Chapter Sixteen

Cotton-ball clouds filled the sky and played cat and mouse with the sun as Keegan pounded the fence post into the ground. Perspiration stuck his shirt to his back, and prior to Fiona's arrival he'd have stripped to the waist to cool himself. He'd have to settle for pouring a bucketful of water over his head.

He shot a glance behind him. She kneeled in front of the cabin, clearing a patch of ground for a flower garden, transforming his place into a home. Another ten days had slipped by since she'd come. No word had been received from the Pinkerton agent tasked with finding Cassie's relatives, so the child remained with them. She played in the shade with her ever-present rag doll. He smiled as he watched her carry on a conversation with the toy.

Fiona's face was shielded by her bonnet, and the gleaming ebony braid that normally hung down her back had been traded for a bun. She'd periodically look over at Cassie, probably to ensure the little girl was safe. Each time her gaze fell on the child, her face bloomed into a smile, love pouring from her eyes.

The fact that she had time to create a garden that did nothing but bring beauty was evidence of her efficiency at running the house. He'd put her up against any farmer's wife in Des Moines, and she made the woman mentioned in Proverbs seem like a layabout. He'd gained a handful of pounds thanks to her cooking, and there was always fresh butter. Cassie had a trunkful of new clothes, and his shirts had all been mended. She'd sewn several throw pillows that added color to the living area. She was currently making some sort of wall hanging with fabric scraps. The vegetable garden had been put in, and sprouts had begun to poke through the soil.

She'd also worked hard at fitting in, and most of the ladies had welcomed her. But slanted looks and conversations that ceased when they approached told him that gossip about her still lingered. Fiona didn't mention it and was gracious to everyone she spoke with, but he could see the lingering hurt in her eyes. Pastor Upton must be aware of the idle talk because this week's sermon addressed the topic in no uncertain terms.

Keegan packed dirt around the post, then rose and carried his tools to the next upright that needed to be replaced. Rot had eaten through the wood on three of the poles, and a strong wind would send them tumbling. A few tugs, and the decaying shaft came loose.

Childish laughter floated toward him, and he turned. Doll abandoned, Cassie had toddled to the garden and dug into the soil with a trowel. Each time she pulled the shovel from the ground, dirt shot into the air and rained down on her and Fiona, who clapped as if the child had performed a momentous feat.

A smile tugged at his lips, and the day seemed brighter. In the trees overhead, a nuthatch warbled. An idea sprang to mind, and he chuckled. With quick motions, he finished installing the new rail, then brushed the dirt from his gloves.

He peeked toward the cabin. Cassie had tired of her so-called helping and had returned to her abandoned doll. Fiona cleared soil from around a rock that stuck up in the middle of the garden. Should he tell her it was probably reminiscent of an iceberg with most of the stone underground? Maybe later. For now, he had a prank to pull.

Hunched over the hole of the last post he needed to repair, he pursed his lips and did his best imitation of a mourning-dove call. Out of the corner of his eye, he saw Fiona stop digging and lift her head. He grinned and wiggled the upright into position. She returned to work. He waited a moment, then repeated the call. Again, she surveyed the area, seeming to search for the elusive bird.

He finished scooping the dirt around the rail, then climbed to his feet. When she resumed her task, he hurried toward the house and circled the structure until he came to the corner closest to where she kneeled. He risked a glimpse and chuckled to himself. She seemed intent on her chore.

Perfect.

After several deep breaths, he puckered his lips and emitted the bird call. He waited a moment, then peeked around the house to watch her reaction. He did this several times until he could barely contain his laughter. One more time, then he'd confess. He craned his neck around the edge of the cabin, then yelped, his heart pounding.

Fiona stood inches away with her hands on her hips, head cocked. Eyes sparkling, her teeth flashed in a wide smile. "Someone doesn't have enough work to do?"

Pressing his hand against his thrumming chest, he snorted a laugh.

She swatted his arm.

Before he could change his mind, he tickled her stomach.

With a squeal, she whirled away from his grip, then picked up her skirts and raced across the yard toward the barn.

Holding back yet staying close enough to catch her if he chose, he ran behind her. He let her get almost inside, then reached out and grabbed her around the waist.

She shrieked and slipped from his grasp. She retreated until her back hit the stall wall. Her eyes widened.

Breathless, he snickered. "Should have watched where you were going."

The patter of feet sounded behind him, and he turned. Cassie trotted into the barn. "Tickle me. Tickle me."

"Don't want to be left out?" He scooped up the child in one arm and poked her belly with the other hand. "How's that?"

Cassie chortled, and his heart swelled. Is this what it felt like to be a father?

Fiona approached, her eyes shining.

He grinned and gave Cassie one more poke before setting her down. He tousled the little girl's hair, and she wrapped one arm around his leg. "I can understand why you took her in. She produces feelings in me I've never had: a fierce protectiveness combined with an urge to make her happy no matter what. 'Tis a shame she'll never know her parents."

"But for now, she has us." Fiona beamed at him, then placed a kiss on his cheek. As she drew back, Cassie tugged on her skirt causing her to stumble against him, her lips brushing the edge of his mouth.

Keegan's pulse raced, and his arms went around her. He breathed her name, then dipped his head and captured her lips with his.

Chapter Seventeen

Fiona melted in Keegan's arms, and her lips softened under his. Her heart thundered against her rib cage as her arms snaked around his waist. He deepened the kiss. Their breath mingled, and she trembled.

Cassie pulled on her skirt. "Mama Fi. What are you doing?"

A chuckle rumbled in Keegan's chest.

She pulled away from him, her face burning. She squatted in front of the little girl, brushing a stray hair out of her face. "Time to wash up, sweetie."

"Okay." Cassie bent and picked up the doll she'd dropped.

Avoiding Keegan's gaze, Fiona grasped the child's hand and led her to the house. Did he think her shameless? Promiscuous? She'd kissed his cheek. If Cassie hadn't caused her to stumble against him, would he have taken the gesture as an invitation. Is that why he kissed her? He thought she wanted it? Had he changed his mind and begun to believe the rumors that Cassie was hers, and that she'd been free and easy with her love.

Tears sprang to Fiona's eyes, and her vision blurred. She blinked them away, then picked up Cassie and rushed inside. He'd laughed as they separated. Was he amused by her discomfiture or responding to the little girl's interruption? It *was* funny in an embarrassing sort of way. Perhaps he wasn't judging her. But what did he think?

She touched her mouth, still tender from the kiss. She could ask Cassie's question of herself. What was she doing? Her body had tingled as soon as their lips connected. Warmth pooled in her stomach, then spread to her limbs. Of their own accord, her arms embraced him, and her toes curled. Did good girls have these reactions to a kiss?

Her chin trembled. If Mama were alive, they could talk about what happened. Madeline had been sweet and welcoming. No, she couldn't talk to her. Her new friend probably thought Fiona's marriage was real at this point. And Keegan would take exception to her discussing their personal lives with someone. She blew out a deep breath. Being married was much more complicated than she'd ever imagined.

Footsteps clomped on the porch, then the door swung open, bringing in sunlight from outside. "Thought you could use some help putting down Cassie for her nap. Maybe read her a story." He cleared his throat. "Keep her mind off things that don't concern her."

Her gaze ricocheted to his face.

He winked and gave her a wry smile.

Tension slipped from her shoulders. He thought the situation was funny. He didn't seem to be censuring her. She released a sigh and nodded. "A wonderful idea." She stroked Cassie's cheek. "Go with Keegan, little one. He's going to read to you. Would you like that?"

Cassie nodded and trotted toward him. "Yay, story."

Scooping her into one arm, he poked her belly.

As they disappeared into the bedroom, Cassie squealed. "Do it again!"

Fiona giggled at the child's excitement, then went to the root cellar to gather produce for dinner. God had certainly worked a miracle since she'd arrived toting Cassie. Keegan had stated in no uncertain terms that he didn't want the little girl, yet he now vowed to adopt her should her true family not be found. *Thank You, Father.*

Keegan's love for Cassie was evident. The child had burrowed her way into his heart.

Rummaging in the bushels, Fiona retrieved potatoes, carrots, and parsnips. Too bad broccoli didn't carry over the winter. She'd have to wait until the garden began to produce before she could have any green vegetables.

She carried the root vegetables back into the kitchen, then grabbed a knife and began to pare the potatoes. The chore didn't require much thought, so her mind went back to the vision of Keegan carting Cassie into the bedroom, and the sound of the little girl's laughter.

"Dear Lord, how long must I wait to see if Cassie will be ours forever? You know the desires of my heart, but would You allow me to love her so much if You weren't going to allow us keep her?"

Patience, My child.

"I'm not good at that, Lord." She sliced the potato and picked up another. "Is that what this is about? Teaching me patience? I'd rather learn it a different way without risking a broken heart."

Trust Me.

Her face flamed. As usual, she was running ahead of her heavenly Father and expecting Him to keep up and follow her lead. When would she stop trying to be in charge?

"I'll do my best." She lifted her chin and smiled. "But I'll need Your help. Like I always do."

She finished preparing the vegetables, then turned on the skillet and placed a small dollop of lard in the pan. Humming, she punched down the dough she'd made first thing this morning and shaped it into a loaf. Why was she surprised that she always felt good after taking her troubles to the Lord? He must get tired of her waffling.

Keegan's voice floated out of the bedroom, rising and lowering as he mimicked the characters in Cassie's storybook. She could listen to him all night. His words had been like warm honey when he'd uttered her name before their kiss. An emotion she couldn't pinpoint flickered in his eyes as they'd pulled apart.

Was he beginning to care for her? Why else would he kiss her? What if he just wanted to test her? See if she was experienced like the rumors said. What had her response told him? She'd leaned into him, embraced him. He must think her quite brazen.

What if her behaviors disgusted him, and he never fell in love with her. Could she be in a marriage like that for the next forty or fifty years? Could she make him fall in love with her? "Mama, I sure wish you were here."

Chapter Eighteen

Keegan unhitched Dolly from the plow and led the horse into the barn. Fiona had asked him to extend the vegetable garden so she could add radishes, broccoli, and cauliflower, and he was happy to oblige. She'd been skittish around him since the kiss and spurned several attempts to discuss the incident. After two days, he'd given up, but he would prefer to know the reason for her behavior. Was she embarrassed? Upset? Disgusted?

She'd hadn't seemed repulsed. In fact, he'd sensed simmering passion before Cassie had interrupted them. He'd give a day's wage to understand women. One woman in particular. His wife. The term rolled awkwardly on his tongue. Would he ever get used to it?

He brushed down the mare, then scooped some oats into the animal's trough. He hung the tack on the wall and checked on the chickens and goats. All was quiet. He'd have time to wash off the day's sweat.

Whether she liked it or not, they needed to have a conversation about what happened. He snorted a laugh. Since when did he talk things out? He hadn't learned the skill at home. His parents either argued or swept the problem under the proverbial rug. But the awkwardness in his home needed to disappear. Soon.

He'd arranged for Madeline to watch Cassie for the afternoon, so he and Fiona could have time alone. As cute and lovable as the little girl could be, she was also demanding, and they'd never be able to have a lengthy discussion in the child's presence. The day was perfect for a wagon ride. The sun was warm without scorching, and a light breeze smelled of summer. Iowa might not be as beautiful as the Emerald Isle, but it held an allure of its own.

Stripping to the waist, he worked the pump until water surged forth. He dunked his head under the cold stream, then soaped up and rinsed off. He shook the water from his hair like Troy, his old Border collie, then toweled dry. He snapped his fingers and frowned. He'd forgotten to retrieve a clean shirt from the house. Rather than don the smelly garment, he wrapped the towel around his shoulders and strode toward the cabin.

Pulse racing at the thought of spending the rest of the afternoon with Fiona, Keegan hurried inside. Back to him, she pulled a pan from the oven. His mouth watered at the aroma of molasses. "You've made gingerbread. Yum."

She set the pan on the counter, then nodded and turned. Her gaze flicked to his bare chest, and her cheeks blazed. She twisted and kneaded the towels she'd used to protect her hands from the hot pan, her eyes ricocheting around the room—anywhere but at him.

He tugged on the towel, trying to cover his skin, but the fabric was too small. He gestured to the bedroom. "I'll grab a clean shirt." He rushed to the bedroom and yanked open the dresser. Grabbing the top garment, he dropped the towel and dressed. He draped the cloth over the door, then sauntered back into the living room.

Wagon wheels sounded in the yard. Good. Madeline had arrived. Before she could knock, he opened the door. She jumped to the ground and approached him with a broad smile. "Is our lady ready to go?"

"I haven't told her."

She giggled. "The element of surprise, eh?"

With a shrug, he stepped back so she could enter. "Fiona, look who's here."

"Madeline." Fiona rushed forward and embraced her friend. "To what do we owe the pleasure? Are you alone?"

"You and Keegan are going on an outing. I'm here to spend time with Cassie."

Fiona's mouth dropped, then her eyebrow lifted, and she whirled toward Keegan. "You planned this?"

"Yes." He ran his finger around his collar. "'Tis a gorgeous day, and I thought we could spend some time together."

Madeline nudged Fiona's shoulder. "Go change your dress. You've a date."

"But—"

"But nothing. I'll take care of the kitchen and Cassie. Don't worry about the house. You've done enough work for one day. Go and relax." She winked. "And get acquainted with your husband."

"Okay." Fiona tossed a glance at him, then scurried into the bedroom and shut the door.

"And you go easy on her." She wagged her finger at him. "She may be from the city, but she's naïve, having spent little time with men. Take my buckboard. There's a basket in the back with food and cider. I expect you to stay out past dinner."

"Thank you. I—"

"I'm happy to do this." She gave him a dismissive wave. "Seamus and I didn't have the added stress of a child in our lives while trying to learn how to be husband and wife. But I meant what I said. Be gentle. Tell her about you and your family. Your hopes and dreams. Let her see the man inside. Give her reasons she should trust you with her heart."

Before he could answer, the bedroom door opened, and Fiona stood on the threshold, a tentative smile on her lips. Her cobalt-colored dress hugged her in all the right places, making her eyes as blue as a summer sky. Her face was tinged a lovely shade of pink. She gripped a small reticule.

Slack-jawed, he stared at her.

Madeline jabbed him. In a stage whisper she said, "Say something."

He blinked and cleared his throat. "You look beautiful."

Fiona ducked her head and murmured, "Thank you."

"Care to join me for a ride?" He crooked his arm. "I know the perfect place for a picnic."

"That would be nice."

"Stop being so polite, you two, and get on out of here!" Madeline shooed them toward the door. "And don't come back until you're comfortable with each other."

Keegan chuckled and put his right hand to his forehead in a mock salute. "You'd give General Meagher a run for his money if he was still alive." He led Fiona outside and helped her settle into the wagon, the feel of her tiny waist still on his hands. He climbed up and dropped beside her. With a flick of his wrist, he got the horse moving, and the wagon lurched forward. They rolled out of the yard and down the lane. "There's a small pond at the far end of the property."

Spine stiff, she clutched her bag and nodded.

"I'm glad to have this time with you. It seems we're always tending to the child."

Her lips thinned, and she remained silent.

"What? 'Tis true."

She blew out a deep breath and studied her hands.

"You have to stay something." He jerked his head back toward the house. "Madeline said—"

"You said you were willing to adopt her, yet everything you say and do seems to indicate you want nothing to do with her. Do you dislike her that much? Dare I say it: hate her?"

"Not at all." His breath exploded, and he raked his fingers through his hair. He spent every evening reading to the little girl. How could she think he hated her? "I'm not sure I can say I love her yet, but I do care for her. However, you've been here a over a month, and we're still virtual strangers. We work at our chores separately, and our meals are spent ensuring she finishes eating. We entertain her until you bathe her, then I put her to bed. After that we're both so tired, we're dead on our feet. The next day we start all over again." He shrugged. "I want to know you. If this marriage is to have any chance at all, I hope you feel the same."

A tear slipped from her eye, and he thumbed away the moisture. His heart clenched. "I didn't mean to make you cry. I've messed up as usual."

"No, this is all my fault. You've been nothing but patient and kind. I'm sorry for assuming how you felt about Cassie." She smoothed her skirts. "I'm pleased she's come to mean something to you."

"But?"

"But what?" Her gaze shifted to the horizon.

"But there's more. Something is bothering you." He didn't want to frighten her, but he risked patting her hand. When she didn't flinch, he laced his fingers with hers and squeezed. "Please, tell me."

Her chin trembled, and she pressed her lips together for a moment. "Are you spending time with me because Madeline told you to?"

"Absolutely not."

"Then why? Are you being nice because you feel sorry for me?"

"No. I want to get to know who you are. You are clever and smart and funny. I enjoy being with you."

"What about the rumors?"

"What about them?"

"Do you believe them?"

"I've told you I don't. Why won't you accept that I'm telling the truth?"

Fiona withdrew her hand from his.

"Whoa." He stopped the wagon and turned, cradling her hands in his palms. "I've apparently not done a good job of showing you that I'm glad you're here. Happy that you're my wife. Have I done something that makes you think I'm a liar? How can we move forward with this marriage if you think I'm untrustworthy?"

Chapter Nineteen

Fiona squinted at the blazing sun overhead, then opened her parasol and sighed. A week had passed since her wagon ride and picnic with Keegan. Temperatures during the last week had been brutally hot day and night. Two brief rainstorms had brought humidity instead of relief. Cassie had developed a case of prickly heat that made her fretful and weepy. Today was the first day the little girl's rash had shown signs of abating, so Keegan had suggested they attend the Independence Day festivities.

Waiting for him to join them after stowing the buckboard in the large field set aside for families coming from outside of town, she surveyed her surroundings. Flags and red, white, and blue bunting hung from windows and rooftops. Streamers dangled from poles and streetlamps. Women's hats had a decidedly patriotic flare, and many men had red or white carnations tucked in their buttonholes. Children scampered through the crowds.

She glanced at the watch pinned to her bodice and frowned. The sidewalk was already lined with people. With her diminutive stature, she'd never be able to view the parade when it started in thirty minutes.

"What a crowd, huh?" Keegan grasped her elbow from behind, his breath brushed her cheek as he spoke.

A shiver feathered down her spine, and she nodded, unable to respond. They'd come to an uneasy truce during their wagon ride. She'd shared her uncertainties and fears about leaving Boston, marrying him, and becoming a farmwife. He'd been gracious and understanding, then talked about his conflicting loyalties between his old country and the new. He was thrilled to be living in America, yet was afraid of losing his identity as an Irishman. His jaw taut, he'd told her about his brother, and she'd seen the mixture of pain and anger in his eyes.

When he'd shared about the heavy-handed laws that prompted he and his friends to protest in efforts to get the British off *his* island, she realized why he struggled with her family's Ulster heritage. With trepidation, she responded that he was no better than the men who claimed her father wasn't a real American.

After that, he'd set the wagon in motion, and they rode in silence for what seemed like hours, but in reality had been perhaps twenty minutes. Finally, when she thought her heart would jump from her chest, he'd brought the buckboard to a halt and apologized. They agreed to start fresh, but residual awkwardness remained.

"Let me carry Cassie, so you don't have to worry about her slipping away in this mob." He lifted the little girl and settled her on his hip. He gestured toward the building across the street. Seamus knows the editor of the newspaper who has agreed to let a few folks watch the parade from the second floor of his place."

"That's wonderful. You've thought of everything."

"We can't have you miss your very first Des Moines parade." He grinned. "Hang on, and I'll get us through."

She closed her parasol, then tucked her hand into the crook of his arm, following him as he plowed through the mass of people. She arrived at the entrance to the newspaper breathless and wide-eyed. Madeline and Seamus waited inside. Keegan closed the door, and the noise subsided to a dull throb. Fiona loosened her bonnet and let it hang down her back. The room was stifling, but at least she wasn't getting jostled or crunched.

"You ladies can head upstairs." Keegan set down Cassie and ruffled her hair. "Seamus and I will go obtain drinks and treats."

"Lovely." Madeline stroked Seamus's cheek, and he brushed a kiss on her mouth. She swatted him on the arm, yet looked pleased. "You're incorrigible."

"And you're beautiful."

She gave him a playful shove. "Get on with you."

Fiona's stomach hollowed. Would Keegan ever act like that with her?

The men clomped out the door, and Madeline turned to her with narrowed eyes. "I saw that look when Seamus kissed me. What gives?"

"Shouldn't we find where we're supposed to be?" Fiona licked her lips. "I'd like to get Cassie settled."

"Follow me, but then we're going to talk about what's going on." She led Fiona and Cassie up the steps and down the hall, then into a large room with several desks. Madeline gestured to the windows that sparkled in the sunlight. "One of the best views of the parade."

"Perfect. They're low enough for Cassie to see out, too."

"Exactly." Madeline crossed her arms. "You and Keegan were awfully quiet when you got home from your picnic, and we haven't had a chance to talk since then. Seamus and I have been praying so hard. Is everything okay?"

Fiona shrugged, and she led Cassie to the windows. "Look outside, little one. See all the people?"

Cassie pressed her nose to the window and giggled. "I see Da!"

Madeline's eyebrow shot up. "Da?"

"Yes, she started calling him that yesterday. I'm Mama Fi." She swallowed past the lump in her throat. "I'm not sure how much longer I can wait to hear from the Pinkerton agency."

"Oh, you poor thing." Madeline rushed forward and drew her into a hug. "We're praying about that, too. How does Keegan feel about her calling him that?"

"He was stunned at first, but I can tell he's pleased."

"Has he declared his feelings for you yet?"

"What?" Fiona reared back. "No."

"But he has them, and so do you."

Fiona began to pace. "Just because he kissed me doesn't mean he has feelings."

"He kissed you?" Madeline squealed and clapped her hands. "Then he must be falling in love with you."

"It was an accident. He didn't mean to."

"To what? Kiss you or fall in love?"

"Kiss me. To make a long story short, I stumbled, he caught me, and we kissed."

"I'd say that was opportunity, not accidental." She beamed. "This is wonderful."

Fiona stopped pacing and put her hands on her hips. "You're making assumptions. Some days are indeed wonderful. We talk and laugh and feel like a family. Then there are other days when everything is awkward and stilted."

"He may not know how to express himself, or he may be unsure of how you feel. If I know Keegan, he doesn't want to put you in a difficult place, and if he declares himself and you don't feel the same, he'll think he's to blame. You have to help him get to a place where he can't help but tell you he's in love."

"That sounds devious."

"Hardly." Madeline grinned and rubbed her hands together. "He watches your every move, and his face lights when you enter a room. He may not know it, but he's in love. Definitely. You just need to make him realize he can't live without you, and that he has no choice but to tell you."

"Tell me what?" Keegan entered the room carrying several bottles of lemonade.

Fiona's heart thundered in her chest. How much had he heard?

The crowd seemed to grow by the second as Keegan followed Seamus down the sidewalk toward the booths that had been set up at the end of Main Street. They'd delivered the drinks, and Fiona studiously avoided his gaze. He and Seamus had obviously interrupted her conversation with Madeline, and both women looked like children caught with their hands in the cookie jar. He knew better than to quiz them, so he and Seamus excused themselves to get the food. What had the girls been discussing?

His mouth watered as savory and sweet aromas mingled in the air. They finally pushed their way clear of the surging celebrants, and he took a deep breath. The surge of humanity was too reminiscent of the protests back in Ireland. He heaved a deep sigh. That life was past.

Seamus stopped at a table where a middle-aged blonde woman sold handheld meat pies. Golden-brown and flaky-looking, the pastries emitted an appetizing fragrance. He dug into his pocket and handed her some coins. "I'll take three, please."

"Certainly." She tucked the money in a small bag that dangled from her waist, then wrapped the food in newspaper.

"Two for me." Seamus paid, and they were soon on their way.

They continued to stroll along the tables, occasionally stopping to make a purchase. Arms laden with food, Keegan grinned. "Looks like we won't be needing dinner tonight." He turned to make his way back to the newspaper office.

"We've enough for two days." Seamus fell in beside him. "So how are things going with you and the new missus?"

Keegan whipped his head toward his friend. "Why? What have you heard?"

"Nothing. That's why I asked."

"Madeline's been over a few times to visit. She hasn't said anything?"

"No. Just that we need to pray for the two of you." He shifted the load in his arms. "It hasn't been so long that I don't remember what it was like with Maddie. The fits and starts. Clumsiness. And more than a few mistakes on both our parts."

"That's about the size of it. I never knew it could be so hard to live with another person, and I've got two, although Cassie has settled into a routine of some sort, so there are times Fiona and I have alone, but we're usually too tired to do much talking."

"Sometimes companionship is all you need." Seamus wiggled his eyebrows. "I see the way you look at her. You're developing feelings for her. That's good."

Keegan nodded. "She's as beautiful on the inside as she is on the outside. But I'm not sure she reciprocates the sentiment. She responded when I kissed her, but it's been awkward ever since."

"You kissed her, eh? Then you did tell her you care."

"No, we...uh...it happened by accident."

Seamus chuckled. "And you wonder at the awkwardness. If I had a free hand, I'd slap you upside the head. You don't kiss a woman without declaring yourself."

"But what if she doesn't feel the same?"

"You need to make her fall in love with you. I'm assuming you both want this marriage to work. Yes?"

"Yes."

"Then approach this as you did in trying to make your farm a success. Only this is more important than that and anything else you'll ever do. Court her, and tell her your intention to do so. She'll appreciate your honesty. Right now, she probably doesn't know what to think...or what you're thinking."

"When did you get to be so wise?"

"A day at a time, my friend." He shook his head. "And by making a lot of mistakes."

"There's something else. I received a telegram yesterday. The Pinkerton agent has found a distant relative of Cassie's. And his wife. I've got to tell Fiona, but I'm dreading the conversation. She's going to be devastated."

"Then this will be an opportunity for you to show you can support her. That she can count on you to help her through the difficult times. You'll be closer as a result. Trust me."

"I don't want to ruin the day."

"If you wait too long, they'll be here."

"I know." He twisted his lips. "I'm the one who pushed for contacting the agency. She's going to hate me."

Chapter Twenty

The traces lay loose in Keegan's palms as the wagon trundled down the road toward home in the inky darkness. Dolly knew the way, so he let the animal amble at her own pace. Fiona dozed against his shoulder, Cassie cuddled in her arms. The day had been full of fun and laughter. They'd watched the parade, window-shopped, listened to the town band perform a concert filled with patriotic music, and stuffed themselves full of food and treats. After an exciting display of fireworks, they'd climbed into the wagon, and the girls had fall asleep within minutes.

He glanced at Fiona. A tendril of hair had escaped her pins and dangled on the side of her face. He took the lock between his fingers, the ebony tress as silky as he imagined it would be. She sighed, and he dropped the hair as if he'd been scalded. He held his breath, but she didn't awaken.

His heart rate slowed, and his shook his head. Seamus was right. He needed to stand up and tell her that he would woo her properly. That he wanted their marriage to be one of love and mutual respect. He'd been a fool, waffling around the emotional aspect of their relationship since she'd arrived. They were married. She deserved to have a marriage in every sense of the word.

But first he needed to tell her about the telegram.

Thirty minutes later, they arrived at his homestead, the cabin and barn dark smudges at the end of the lane. "Fiona, wake up. We're nearly home."

She sat up and blinked, her neck swiveling as she took in her surroundings. "Home?"

"Yes. You slept for most of the journey. How do you feel?"

"Groggy." She yawned and pulled Cassie closer. "I'm sorry you had no company for the ride. I didn't realize I was so tired."

He guided the wagon to a stop in front of the house. "Having fun is exhausting."

She giggled, the sound like silver bells at Christmastime.

"Would you like help putting Cassie to bed? Dolly can wait a few minutes to be taken care of."

"No, I'll be fine, but I wouldn't mind some coffee."

"Deal." He jumped down, then took Cassie from her so she could climb out of the conveyance. She reached for the child, murmuring to her as they entered the house. Yes, Fiona was going to be hurt at the news. He shoved his hat off his forehead and led Dolly to the barn. Minutes later, the horse had been unhitched, rubbed down, and fed. He gave the mare one last pat, then hurried toward the cabin.

He stepped inside and cocked his head. Fiona's voice filtered out of the bedroom. He crept to the door and peeked inside. She knelt on the floor next to the bed, head bowed and fingers laced as she prayed. Propped against a pillow, Cassie mimicked her posture, her eyes screwed shut.

His heart swelled. God had surely blessed him. He tiptoed to the kitchen and prepared the coffee. She'd need it strong to hear his news. He grabbed a pair of mugs and set them next to the stove, then dropped into a chair at the table. *Give me the right words, Father, and please prepare her.*

Several minutes later, Fiona closed the door to the bedroom. She lifted her chin and sniffed. "That smells wonderful."

"The brew that cures all ills."

"I agree, although Mother tried to convert me to a tea drinker."

He stood and held one of the chairs for her. As she sat down, the clean scent of her hair wafted toward him. He found the urge to lean down and take a deep breath. Instead, he poured their drinks, then sat beside her. "I've got news."

Fiona paled, and her eyes pooled with moisture. "They've found a relative."

"I'm afraid so." He laced her fingers in his and rubbed his thumb in a circle on the back of her hand. "A second cousin. He's married with children of his own."

Her chin trembled, and she blinked away the tears. "Family is important. Blood. That's what matters. I'm glad for her. She'll grow up with her own."

"Yes, but I'm sorry for you. For us." He squeezed her hand. "I know you love her very much."

"I do." Her voice broke. "But they will love her more. At least I hope they will."

Please God, let it be so. He wouldn't mention the family back in Ireland who'd taken in a niece and nephew and treated them no better than servants.

Sniffling, she extracted her hand from his, then pulled a hanky from her pocket and dabbed at her eyes. She stowed the linen cloth, picked up her mug, and took another sip. "When will they be arriving?"

"Uh, tomorrow." He rubbed the back of his neck. Here's where she'd get thick as a bull about the last-minute notice. No doubt she'd want time to clean and prepare to say nothing of having more time with Cassie.

Fiona pushed herself to her feet. "We've a lot of work to do and not much time to do it." She laid her hand on his shoulder. "Thank you for all you're doing for Cassie's good." She trudged to the cedar chest and lifted the lid.

Keegan downed the rest of his coffee while she pulled the little girl's clothing from the chest. Fiona hadn't reacted at all as he'd anticipated. She was disappointed, hurt, and upset, but she'd held her emotions in check. She'd recognized that the move was for the child's best interest. Painful, but necessary. His wife had depths he hadn't seen until now. He didn't deserve her.

Chapter Twenty-One

Swollen, gray clouds scudded across the sky, and Fiona pulled her cloak tighter around her and Cassie. A cold breeze tugged at her bonnet. Would the rain hold off long enough for them to arrive at the train station to meet the child's cousin? Was the storm God's way of grieving with her?

She rubbed her slick palms on her skirt and took several deep breaths to calm her thundering heart. Keegan glanced at her, and she sent him what she hoped was a brave smile. He'd complimented her on her response yesterday, telling her how proud he was of her. Little did he know the myriad emotions that battled inside her heart. She'd prayed for forgiveness through the night for her anger at God allowing the relatives to be found and pressed her face against the pillow to stifle her sobs. Deep down, she knew Cassie living with family was for the best, but did that knowledge mean Fiona had to like it?

Keegan had been gracious all morning, rushing through his chores so he could be in the house with her. He'd teased her unmercifully between playing and reading to Cassie in obvious attempts to keep up her spirits. She loved how comfortable he'd become with the little girl.

Wait. Love?

Her pulse skipped. Memories of the last few weeks swam into her mind. Keegan curled up with a book and Cassie on his lap. Keegan drying the dishes beside her, eyes twinkling and a sloppy grin on his face. Keegan helping her in the vegetable garden, the motions causing the muscles under his shirt to ripple. Keegan sitting beside her at church intent on the preacher's words. Keegan holding her chair at the dinner table. Keegan seeming to hang on her every word when they talked about everything and nothing.

Yes, she did love him even though only a few short weeks had passed since her arrival. Suddenly aware of how close they perched together on the buckboard, she froze. Could he feel the heat that shimmered between them? Or was she imagining the warmth that emanated from his wiry form.

He'd not pushed for a physical relationship, although as her husband he had the right. Was he tired of waiting, or did he not desire her? If Madeline was to be believed, he did care for her at some level. Was affection all that was necessary for him to want to share her bed? Her mouth dried at the vision of him entering the bedroom. Mum had told her very little about the intimate aspect of marriage, her fumbling attempts embarrassing them both.

But if Fiona wanted children, she would have to share his bed. She risked a glance at him and found him staring, a look of concern on his face. She forced a smile.

He nudged her shoulder. "I'm sorry for how difficult this is for you."

She pulled Cassie closer to her, and the child sighed. "In my mind, I keep chanting 'God knows best.'"

"That He does, but sometimes His best hurts as He grows and shapes us."

The shriek of the train's whistle split the air as the wagon rolled into the station. Tears sprang to her eyes, and she blinked them away. She must be strong.

Keegan jumped down from the conveyance. "Hopefully, I won't be long." He melted into the crowd, then returned too soon, leading a man and woman who appeared to be around her age. Somehow, she'd expected them to be older. Or perhaps she only wished it so she could prove they shouldn't take Cassie.

Tall and good-looking with dark hair and eyes, the man was the antithesis of his petite wife whose white-blonde hair and blue eyes gave her a regal air. The man bowed. "You must be Fiona. I'm Hugh Sandell, and this is Pearl. Thank for taking care of my cousin's daughter."

Fiona pinned on a smile and pulled back her cloak to reveal Cassie. "This is Cassie, and it has been a joy."

Keegan tossed their satchels into the back of the wagon, then gestured for them to climb aboard. "You must be hungry. There is a wonderful diner close by."

"That sounds lovely. If you'll point the way, we'll meet you there. We'd like to stretch our legs after being on the train."

"Oh, of course." Keegan gestured north. "Turn right down Main Street, and the café is five or six doors down. It's called Grub and Goodies."

"Thank you." The man bowed again, then slipped his wife's hand through the crook in his arm. "We'll see you in a few minutes."

"We look forward to it." Keegan got into the wagon and dropped beside Fiona as the couple ambled away.

"Why didn't they want to ride with us? Do you think they're disappointed? They seem to have a lot of money. Maybe they think they're saving Cassie from a life of poverty."

Keegan wrapped his arm around her shoulder. "Relax. They've been on a train for two days. I'd want to take a walk after that, too."

She huffed a sigh. "You're right. I just want things to be perfect. I want them to like us...and Cassie."

"And they will." He released her and clicked his teeth. "Hyah." The wagon lurched forward, and moments later they were in front of the diner. He tied the horse to the rail, and the three of them headed inside to secure a table at the cozy restaurant.

Seated in the corner, Fiona jiggled her leg and her chest tightened. Her gaze was riveted to the door, yet she startled when the couple appeared in the doorway.

They wended their way through the tables and sat in the vacant chairs across from Fiona. Pearl patted her hair. "We've never been to Des Moines. The town is bigger than we anticipated."

Keegan nodded. "And growing larger by the day."

The waitress, a young woman from church whose name escaped Fiona, came over and took their orders. She studied the Sandells with interest, but to Fiona's relief didn't ask any questions. Minutes later she was back with four steaming mugs of coffee and a cup of water.

"How was—"

"We—"

Nervous laughter bubbled up from Fiona, and Keegan cradled her hand. Trying to show her support, he didn't know how his touch affected her.

He dipped his head to the couple. "Go head."

Mr. Sandell smiled. "We wanted to let you know how grateful we are for you taking in my cousin's child. I never met either one of them, being distantly related through our mothers, but family is family."

"Indeed." Keegan sipped his coffee. "Do you have children?"

Mrs. Sandell beamed. "Three with one on the way. We've just got the news from my doctor before coming here."

"Congratulations." Fiona's voice sounded flat in her ears. Cassie would be one of five kids. Would she get lost in the crowd? How would the others treat her? "Did you always want a big family?"

The couple exchanged a look she couldn't decipher. Mrs. Sandell shrugged. "To be honest, we hadn't talked about it, and for the first five years of our marriage I didn't conceive, so we thought children weren't in our future." Her face pinked. "Then I became pregnant, and we've had a child each year."

"Thank you for your candor." Fiona swallowed. "Proper society normally doesn't discuss this topic, but I appreciate you telling us."

"You want to know if Cassie is going to a good family."

"Not that it's any of my business, but yes." Fiona rubbed at the rim of her cup. "I would hate for her to go somewhere she's not wanted."

"We understand."

Cassie fidgeted and rubbed her eyes. She tugged at Fiona's sleeve. "I not hungry."

"How about a drink of water?"

Shaking her head, the little girl crossed her arms and pressed her lips together. "Not thirsty. I want to play."

"Sometimes we have to do things we don't want. We can play after we talk with these nice people."

She looked mulish.

Fiona swallowed a sigh. Would the Sandells think she had done a poor job resulting a stubborn child?

"She reminds me of our youngest." Mrs. Sandell chuckled. "How about if Fiona and I take her for a quick walk down the sidewalk until our food arrives."

"Won't we be giving in to her demands?"

"We're not going to play, just take a breather. That often works with our son."

"You sound like a pro at this."

Mrs. Sandell rose. "Hardly."

Fiona pushed to her feet and grabbed Cassie's hand. They followed the woman from the restaurant. Outside, the weather had cleared. The gray clouds had been replaced by clear blue skies and sunshine. Cassie reached for Mrs. Sandell's hand, and the child skipped between them as they strolled down the wooden sidewalk.

"She seems well-adjusted. You've done a wonderful job with her."

"Thank you. She was fretful in the beginning not understanding about her parents' deaths. I wish I had a photograph she could carry with her through life. I don't want her to forget them."

"It is a shame, but we will tell her what we know of them, keeping them alive in her heart."

They reached the end of the block and pivoted. Fiona cleared her throat. "You are very kind to take her with so many children of your own."

"You have no children yet?"

Fiona dropped her gaze. "I'm a mail-order bride. I met Cassie and her parents on my way here."

"Goodness. I've never met a real mail-order bride." Mrs. Sandell squinted at her. "I assume your groom didn't expect you to come with a child in tow."

"Hardly, but he's adjusted. In fact, he's grown quite attached to Cassie."

"Then he will make a wonderful father."

They entered the restaurant and threaded their way to the table.

"I love Fiona and will do anything to make her happy." Keegan finger-combed his hair. "I assume you feel the same about your wife."

Fiona froze as his words swept over her.

Keegan continued, "You need to determine if taking Cassie is the right decision for your family, not just doing it to fulfill an obligation. If I learned nothing over the past few weeks, it's that family isn't always about blood."

She exchanged a look with Fiona. Keegan knew how much she wanted to keep Cassie. Was he claiming love for Fiona as a way to sway the Sandells? Or did he really have feelings for her? Did she want to know the answer?

Chapter Twenty-Two

Despite the early morning hour, the temperature already hovered just below scorching. Perspiration plastered Keegan's shirt to his back, and moisture trickled down the sides of his face as he finished his chores. Even the chickens were lethargic, milling about their pen rather than performing their frantic dance while pecking the ground for food. The heat magnified the earthy aromas in the barn to an eye-watering level.

He wiped his hands on a rag, then ambled to the house where he grabbed the soap, towel, and clean shirt he'd left on the porch. His boots sent up swirls of dust as he walked to the pump. Except for the lump of soap, he tossed the items on the ground a safe distance away, then worked the handle until water surged from the nozzle. He dunked his head and torso under the stream, lathering his hair and body in the frigid spray.

Clean and refreshed, he toweled off before donning his cotton shirt. He'd argued with himself as to how dressed up he needed to be to take Fiona and Cassie into town to meet the Sandells and chose to forgo formal wear. The couple had come to the house yesterday to announce their decision to take the little girl into their family. Fiona had controlled her emotions until after the child was bedded down for the night. His heart heavy, he'd held his wife while she cried, wishing the outcome had been different, but pleased she allowed him the intimacy of an embrace. After she calmed down, they prayed together, beseeching God to help them accept the loss, and the act brought him even closer to Fiona. Did she feel the same?

The front door opened, and she appeared on the threshold carrying Cassie on her hip. "You about ready?"

"As I'll ever be." He hung the towel and his soiled shirt on the railing. "Am I presentable?"

Her cheeks pinked, and she nodded. "I like that shirt."

"Brings out the blue in my eyes." He batted his eyelashes. "Don't you think?"

She snickered, then sobered up. "I've got everything packed, and put together a food basket for them."

"I'm sure they'll appreciate the gesture." He slipped past her and grabbed the satchel and basket filled with fragrant bundles. "This should hold them for a while. Give me a few minutes to hitch the wagon." He hurried to the barn and hoisted the items into the buckboard, then coaxed Dolly from her stall, put on her tack, then attached the traces to the wooden tongue. He led the mare into the yard, squinting in the dazzling sunlight. "Be sure to grab your parasol or you'll be burned by the time we arrive at the station."

Handing Cassie to him, Fiona went back inside and returned with the cotton umbrella. She climbed into the wagon, and he set the little girl in her lap. She opened the parasol and sighed. "Boston was never this hot."

"Wait until August. You'll be pining for July." He clicked his teeth, and the mare moved forward. They rolled away from the house and down the lane toward the road that would take them to town and the next chapter of their lives: one without the sweet little girl he'd grown to adore.

They rode in silence for miles, and he reveled in Fiona's proximity. What could he do to make things better for her? Gifts wouldn't erase the pain, and activities would only make her forget for a while. What would get her mind off losing Cassie?

He glanced at her, and she smiled at him through tear-filled eyes. His stomach hollowed. She'd burrowed her way into his heart. Should he tell her? In the few weeks since she entered his life, it seemed as if she might care for him, too. Just a bit. But was it enough? Dare he ask her if she was ready to live as man and wife so he could give her what she desired most: a child.

Not that she'd forget Cassie, but perhaps a baby of her own would ease the ache. His palms slicked. Would she be insulted by a request to share her bed? Frightened? Disgusted? And when should he make such an overture?

The edge of town came into view, and he huffed a deep breath. Focus, man. Fiona stiffened beside him, and he sent her what he hoped was an encouraging smile. "We're in this together. And God is with us."

She lifted her chin. "That He is. Thank you for the reminder. I'm struggling not to grab the reins and turn this contraption toward home."

"Just say the word." He winked. "We will get through this."

Moments later, they came to the station, steam enveloping the eastbound train. Mr. and Mrs. Sandell stood on the platform, their expressions inscrutable. Did they rue their decision? Could he change their mind? He helped Fiona out of the wagon, then put his arm around her waist, and she leaned into him, her steps tentative. He dipped his head in acknowledgment of Mr. Sandell's wave. "Good morning. Ready to go, I see."

"Yes, yes. Our bags are on board." The man exchanged glances with his wife. "Thank you for all you've done for Cassie. You've gone above and beyond the call of duty."

Keegan cleared his throat. "Speaking of duty...uh...you don't need to take her out of a sense of obligation. We'll understand if adding one more child to your expanding family is too much. We're happy to raise her as our own."

"No." Mrs. Sandell shook her head. "She belongs with us, but thank you for the offer." She held out her arms.

Chin trembling, Fiona kissed Cassie on the cheek, then passed her to the woman.

Cassie wailed and twisted in Mrs. Sandell's grasp. She reached for Fiona, her face red and mottled. Tears streamed down her cheeks. "Mama Fi!"

"I-I'm sorry," Fiona's voice cracked. "I can't watch her leave." She pulled away from him and raced down the sidewalk.

"Fiona!" He turned back to the Sandells. "I—"

"Go see to your wife." Mr. Sandell gestured to Fiona's disappearing form. "We'll send a telegram when we arrive home safely."

"Thank you." Keegan rushed in the direction she'd run, threading his way through the foot traffic. He caught sight of her bonnet, then watched in horror as she darted into the street in front of an oncoming carriage.

Chapter Twenty-Three

The minutes on the mantel clock trudged forward. Fiona blew out a sigh, then shifted on the couch and winced as pain shot from her ankle to her hip. She'd been a fool and lucky she hadn't been killed for yesterday's actions. Perhaps not luck, more like God protecting her from herself.

Fortunately, the driver of the carriage was alert, or she'd be lying in the cemetery instead of the cabin. A severe sprain is what the doctor had diagnosed. If this was a sprain, she'd hate to break a bone. Her ankle was the size of a cantaloupe and the color of her favorite purple gown. Would she ever wear the dress again without thinking of her stupidity?

She'd missed saying goodbye because of being overcome with sadness. She'd let down Cassie at the moment when the child needed her most. Is that why God had allowed her to be taken? Did He know Fiona wasn't ready for full-time motherhood?

Her eyes welled with tears. She claimed to trust Him, but her actions said otherwise. He knew what was best for her. The Bible never promised a pain-free road as one of God's followers, but He would walk beside her or carry her if necessary. She cast a glance at the ceiling. "Did You allow me to get hurt so the physical ache would distract me from my breaking heart? Or maybe You put me on my back, so I could look up to You. Or maybe You're just using the opportunity to get my attention. Whatever the reason, Father, please forgive me for failing to rely on You."

Warmth like a blanket settled on her shoulders, and she smiled. *Thank You, Lord.*

Cassie had lived with Keegan and her for six weeks. Enough time to teach her what it meant to be a parent. She should be grateful for the chance to learn and to guide the little girl. The pain would recede until the memories were bittersweet rather than distressing. Meanwhile, she should look to the future. A future that would include children of her own.

Her face flamed. When would that happen? "Stop, Fiona. You're rushing ahead. Again. God's in control." Mama would tell her to stop wallowing. She'd been six or seven the first time her mother used the expression about Fiona's sulking. She hadn't gotten her way about something...probably snacking between meals...nothing important, for sure, and she had plunked herself in the corner waiting for Mama to relent. Which never happened.

"Oh, Mama, I wish you were here. You were so strong, even in your last days."

I'm with you, My child.

Fiona grinned. "Thank You, Lord. I should stop *wallowing*, shouldn't I? Time to get up and make myself useful." She rubbed her hands together. "Baking always makes me feel better. A chocolate cake is in order."

With a deep breath, she swung her feet to the floor. Her vision swam, and she closed her eyes against the swirling. Her head cleared. "All right. Let's do this." She gripped the arm of the sofa and put her weight on her uninjured foot, keeping her bad leg above the floor. "So far, so good." She reached for the T-shaped stick the doctor had given her. A clever contraption that fit under her arm to keep her upright, it was the perfect height for her. She hopped toward the kitchen, wincing each time she came down.

Breathing heavily, she grabbed the back of the closest chair. Perspiration trickled down her back and pooled under her arms. She used her sleeve to blot the moisture from her hairline. Digging the garden had been easier than this.

After resting, she leaned on the crutch and hopped to the kitchen. She leaned on the counter with a triumphant smile, her heart pounding. The ankle's swelling had reduced somewhat, and the knifelike pain was gone. She lit the stove and set to work pulling out the ingredients for the cake.

Madeline had encouraged her to do things for Keegan, and chocolate was his favorite. Would he notice her efforts? Would the simple act of making him a cake turn his heart toward hers? She'd overheard him profess his love of her to Mr. Sandell, but how true was the claim? Was he trying to use emotion to sway the couple about their decision to keep Cassie?

"I'm borrowing trouble again, Father." She sighed and beat the sugar and lard together, then retrieved a couple of eggs from the bowl and cracked them into the mixture. "But I do love him. I've realize that now. And I don't want to be alone in our marriage. I don't want to be the only one of us in love. Please turn his heart toward me, if it isn't already, and help me be patient until that time comes."

She added the remaining ingredients and stirred, her mind twirling as fast as her spoon. "I'll make a pot roast, too. And put candles and a cloth on the table for dinner. And don my best Sunday dress. Won't he be surprised." She poured the batter into a pan and slid it into the oven. "He'll return to find a cheerful wife."

Humming, Fiona made the frosting, then sat down to rest. She plucked at her bodice that clung to her body with perspiration. Yes, she would definitely need to change her clothes. And take a sponge bath. She glanced at the watch pinned to her dress. Time to take out the cake and get to work on dinner. Hobbling around had made the tasks take nearly twice as long. At this rate they'd be eating at midnight.

A laugh bubbled up. Keegan wouldn't be as impressed if that happened. Bracing herself on the crutch, she rose. She hopped forward, but the stick caught in her skirts, and she swayed. She lost her balance and dropped the crutch. Her arms pinwheeled, and her injured foot slammed into the ground. Excruciating pain exploded in her ankle. Nausea swept over her, and pinpoints of light sparkled her vision.

She tottered forward, and her head hit the edge of the table.

Everything went black.

Chapter Twenty-Four

Keegan whistled as he approached the cabin. Yesterday had been rough, but today had dawned bright and fair, and Fiona seemed to be on the mend. Seeing her nearly killed by an oncoming carriage had been terrifying. She'd been embarrassed, but he assured her he understood her distraction because of her devastation over Cassie leaving. With her supine on the couch for the remainder of the day, he'd had an excuse to wait on her and spend extra time with her.

To take her mind off the child's absence, he regaled Fiona with stories from Ireland. Accounts from his growing-up years as well as the myths and legends that pervaded the country. He'd been stunned at her lack of familiarity with them. One generation removed from the Emerald Isle, and she knew little of her heritage. Had her parents been ashamed, or was life so bad they turned their back on their former homeland? She'd mentioned her father's desire to prove himself an American by enlisting to fight in the war. Did the man think that by speaking of their culture and traditions he was being disloyal to his new country? What a shame.

She enjoyed the tales and quizzed him extensively for information. He looked forward to telling her more, perhaps even taking a voyage to visit Mum and Da. Introducing her to the gorgeous island. It would take a long time to save for such a trip but would be worth it.

"Fi—"

The couch was empty. Was she in the bedroom?

"Fiona?" He marched to the bedroom and opened the door. Vacant. Had she tried to go to the outhouse on her own? Limping across the uneven terrain of the backyard with only a crutch to help? He should have come inside sooner to help her.

His gaze swept the small room. A fragrant chocolate cake sat on the counter next to a bowl and a collection of ingredients. She'd managed to make a cake? He strode around the table to the stove and nearly stumbled over her prone form.

"Fiona!"

Her ashen complexion and a gash on the side of her head brought his heart to his throat. Was she dead? He dropped to his knees and laid his fingers to her neck as he'd seen doctors do in the past. Erratic bumping told him she was still alive. "Thank You, God."

He bent and kissed her cheek. "Fiona? Wake up, honey. You hit your head."

Nothing. Her eyes remained closed, her breathing shallow.

"Fiona? Please God, help me get her to the doc on time so he can save her." Keegan jumped to his feet and ran into the bedroom to grab a clean shirt. He wouldn't risk using a dirty kitchen towel on her wound. He didn't know anything about healing people, but he'd sustained enough injuries to know cleanliness was crucial. Too bad he wasn't a drinking man. He'd also seen doctors pour liquor on cuts to sanitize them.

He tore the shirt into strips, then folded one of the pieces into a small square and pressed it to her scalp. Holding the fabric into place with one hand he wrapped another strip around her head to hold the bandage in place.

What if she never woke up?

His pulse skittered. "Stop. You can't think like that." He lifted her into his arms and brushed a kiss on her cheek. Her skin was soft and silky but cold to his lips. Was life already ebbing from her?

"Please, Lord, don't take her from me. I love her too much to lose her." He put her on the couch, then raced to the barn to saddle Dolly. He'd carry Fiona to Seamus's place, then head to town for the doctor. Surely, that would be better than jostling her on a horse all the way into Des Moines. He led the horse to the front of the house, then ran inside, picked her up, and carried her to the animal. His muscles protested as he tried to mount without dropping her. Finally settled with Fiona curled against his chest, he nudged Dolly forward.

He cradled her still form and stroked her back as he gripped the reins one-handed. The need for speed warred with the desire to keep from harming her further. Alternately murmuring in her ear and begging God to save her, he covered the miles quicker than he'd hoped.

"Seamus! Madeline!" He brought the horse to a stop. "Help."

The door flew open, and his friends rushed toward him. Madeline's eyes widened. "Oh, no. Fiona. What happened?"

"I don't know. I found her on the floor. She may have tripped or fainted, but whatever happened, she hit her head."

Seamus reached up and took Fiona from him. "You stay here with her. I'll get the doctor."

The tightness in Keegan's chest eased. "Thank you."

They hurried into the house, and Seamus carried her to the bedroom and laid her on top of the mattress. He pulled the quilt over her, then squeezed Keegan's shoulder. "I'll be back as soon as I can. Pray the doctor is in his office." He tiptoed from the room, and seconds later the front door closed.

Madeline came in carrying a bowl of water and some rags. "Grab a chair from the kitchen so you can sit beside her while I clean the wound."

"Is that safe? Shouldn't we wait for the doctor?"

"No, I've had to fix up enough of the ranch hands, I know what I'm doing. You'll find a bottle of whiskey under the sink. Bring that, too."

He gaped at her.

"For her head." She jerked her head toward the door. "Hurry. There's no time to waste."

His heels clattered on the wooden floor as he did as Madeline bade him. By the time he returned to the bedroom, she'd removed his makeshift bandage and was dabbing at Fiona's scalp with firm motions. The water was a murky red. His stomach roiled, and he looked away. Since when was he squeamish?

"It's different when someone you love is hurt." Madeline held out her hand for the bottle. "Seat yourself on the other side of the bed and hold her hand. Talk to her. Tell her she'd going to be fine. Who knows if she can hear us, but I'd like to think she can."

Plunking down the chair, he lowered himself and engulfed her hand in both his palms. Could she feel that? "I'm here, Fiona. Seamus went for the doctor, and Madeline's doing a great job of taking care of you." His eyes welled with tears, and his voice broke. "We'll see you through this. I promise."

"You're doing great." Madeline poured a generous amount of the liquor onto a cloth, then held it against the gash for a moment. "That should do it until the doc can look at her." She wrapped a clean bandage around Fiona's head. "I'll keep watch for Seamus."

Without taking his eyes off his wife, he nodded. He squeezed her hand, then rose and pressed his lips against hers. "I love you, Fiona. Please come back to me." He laid his forehead on the bed and prayed as he'd never prayed before.

Time passed, and commotion outside told him Doc Lambert had arrived. He leaped up as the man rushed into the room, Seamus and Madeline on his heels. "She's still unconscious."

"Madeline will help me, boys, and you can wait in the living room." As he spoke, the doctor set his leather satchel on the floor, then shed his jacket.

Keegan froze in place.

"I won't be long." Dr. Lambert rolled up his sleeves. "I'll do my best by her."

He bent and kissed Fiona again, then hurried from the room.

Seamus stood in front of the fireplace holding out a small envelope. "I passed Gopher from the telegraph office on my way to the doctor. He was headed to your place with it."

"A telegram?" Keegan took the envelope in trembling fingers. Had something happened to one of his parents? He ripped open the flap and yanked out the folded sheet of paper. His gaze drank in the words, and he smiled. "The first good news in two days."

Chapter Twenty-Five

What is that noise? Where am I? Fiona opened her eyes, then slammed them shut as glare from the window pierced her vision. Since when did she lie down in the middle of the day? Her head throbbed, and her body ached. Pressure on her fingers. Gentle snoring.

She cracked one eyelid.

Keegan sat on a wooden chair, his hand encompassing hers, and his head propped on the mattress beside her. Sunlight glistened on his reddish-blond hair. Her hand itched to stroke the fiery strands to see if they were as soft and warm as they appeared.

But she didn't have the right to touch him. Not like that. Not yet. Maybe not ever. Her lips trembled, and she sighed. Touching her head, she felt the bandage. Exploring further, her fingers came across the bump, and she winced. How had she managed to hurt herself? Was her injury serious? Is that why she was in bed?

But where?

Opening both eyes, she surveyed the room. It wasn't the cozy place she occupied in Keegan's cabin. No rough-hewn walls. No pine dresser with a pink-and-white-ceramic pitcher and bowl. No blue nine-patch quilt.

The pencil-post bed and matching nightstands spoke of wealth. A full-length, framed mirror stood in one corner, a rocking chair in the other. Gauzy white curtains graced the windows. She'd seen curtains like this in the past, but where?

Her mind sifted through her memories. Madeline had living-room sheers like this. Was she at Madeline's home? If so, why? The haziness began to clear from her brain. A cake. She'd baked a cake for Keegan. Dinner had been next, but she'd fallen. Clumsy as ever, she'd tripped over her skirts. She must have hit her head at some point. He must think her an idiot.

If she continued to do foolish things, he'd never fall in love with her. She'd be alone in her feelings. Could she live out the rest of her life in a one-sided relationship?

Tears welled in her eyes, then coursed down her cheeks. She pressed her lips together to keep from giving into full-fledged sobbing. Pressure built in her chest, and she sniffled.

Keegan's head jerked up. A smile bloomed on his face. "You're awake." He squeezed her fingers, then stroked her jaw. "How do you feel? You've been asleep for hours."

Her skin tingled, and she dropped her eyes to avoid his intense blue gaze. "Like I fell from a hayloft."

"Everything hurts, does it?" He cradled her hand in his. "The doctor says you're going to be fine, but you gave us a right scare, you did."

"I'm sorry." She blinked away more tears. She'd turned into a crybaby. "I just wanted to do something nice for you."

"The cake. It's still on the counter." His voice caressed her. "Why won't you look at me? There's no reason to be embarrassed."

She peeked at him from under her lashes. His eyes sparkled, and his expression was filled with...love? No, that wasn't possible. She shrugged.

"Accidents happen." One corner of his mouth lifted in a lopsided grin, and he wagged his finger at her in mock anger. "Especially when one doesn't obey doctor's orders, and thinks she cook dinner while standing on one leg. You didn't even give yourself a day to heal."

"I was feeling useless. You were in the barn getting chores done, and I was on the couch taking up space."

"Ah, Fiona, always trying to prove yourself. 'Tisn't necessary. Don't you know, I've grown to love you because of who you are, not because of what you can do for me." His cheeks reddened. "I care about the woman you are inside: generous, smart, witty, and faithful to our God."

"You love me?" Her eyes widened, and her pulse raced. His claims to Mr. Sandell had been true. "You really love me?"

Keegan chuckled and cocked his head. "Is that so hard to believe?"

"I dared not hope," she whispered. "I thought I was alone in my feelings."

"Then you love me, too?"

"With all my heart."

He leaned toward her, eyes cloudy. "I want to kiss you, but don't want to cause you pain."

"I'm willing to take the risk." She extricated her hand and cupped the back of his neck, drawing him toward her.

Sliding his arms around her, he pressed his lips on hers, firm yet gentle.

A sigh escaped, and she melted into his embrace, giving fully of herself. His grasp tightened, and she reveled in the joy.

He lifted his head, kissed the tip of her nose, then grabbed her hands as he sat next to her on the mattress. "I've got news that will brighten your day."

"More than the discovery that you love me?" She sent him a saucy smile. "What could be better than that?"

"I'll let you see for yourself." He released her hands and dug into his shirt pocket, then held out a small, folded piece of paper. "We received a telegram."

"Telegrams rarely bring good news." She took the note and opened it. Her gaze absorbed the words, but her mind refused to believe them. She raised her eyes to Keegan.

He nodded. "God has worked a miracle. Cassie is coming home to us."

"Oh, Keegan. We're going to be a family." Fiona threw her her arms around him. "I can hardly wait. When does she arrive?"

"The day after tomorrow."

"We've much to do to prepare." She started to swing her legs over the bed, but he stayed her movement.

"There's plenty of time, but first we must see if the doctor thinks you're strong enough to go home."

"Just a small headache." She laid her hand on his chest, feeling the steady thump of his heart under her fingers. Leaning forward, she stopped a hairsbreadth away from his mouth. "When we get there I can show you just how well I've recovered."

One year later

Epilogue

Cassie squealed and pointed out the window at the parade in the street below. Fiona smiled and exchanged a glance with Keegan. He winked, his gaze falling to her lips. Her toes curled, and warmth spread from her belly to the tips of her fingers. If she wasn't careful, she'd drop three-month-old Eoin, named in honor Keegan's brother.

The infant gurgled and waved his fist as if he, too, was excited about the Independence Day celebrations. She stroked his downy, golden-red hair, then kissed his forehead, breathing in his powdery baby scent. *Thank You, God.*

"Mama Fi! Look!" Cassie jumped up and down. "Pwetty."

Music floated up to the newspaper offices as the town band marched down Main Street ahead of a line of wagons festooned with banners, flags, and signs. Buckboards had been transformed by organizations and individuals into vignettes declaring their patriotism. The town had already created a committee to plan the festivities for the country's centennial in two years.

So much had occurred in the last year. What would two more years bring? More children?

This season's crops were already abundant, which meant more money in the coffers to visit Keegan's parents in Ireland. They'd exchanged numerous letters, and his mum and da had welcomed her with open arms. Keegan was sure they'd take exception to marrying a girl whose heritage rested in Ulster, but they'd quickly assured him that if he loved her, then they did, too.

A traveling photographer had come through town, and Keegan splurged on having their picture taken so he could send one to his parents and hang another above the fireplace. She never tired of looking at their little family captured in time.

Gentle fluttering quivered in her middle, and smiled. Yesterday, the doctor had confirmed what she suspected: there would be another member of the family next winter. She peeked at Keegan, and her cheeks heated. He stared at her, his eyes were dark with longing. Putting his fingers to his mouth, he blew her a kiss. She grinned and pretended to catch it.

"Don't you two lovebirds ever quit?" Seamus rolled his eyes as he entered the room.

Keegan snorted a laugh. "No, and you're one to talk."

"True." He held out a telegram. "I was passing the mercantile, and Gopher ran this out to me knowing I'd see you at some point."

Fiona's pulse tripped, and she hurried to Keegan's side.

He tore open the flap, pulled out the folded paper, and held it so she could read over his shoulder:

SOLD COTTAGE AND BOAT. COMING TO STAY. WILL ARRIVE JULY 25.

—LOVE DA

Enveloping her in his arms, Keegan whooped and danced her around the room. Cassie shrieked and raced to join them. He bent and lifted the little girl into his embrace, and the three of them sashayed and cavorted across the wooden floor.

Seamus clapped his hands and cheered. "Wonderful news, friend. We'd be happy to put up your folks until they find a place to stay."

Breathless, Fiona stopped dancing. "They'll stay with us, of course. We can use the money we were saving for the voyage to build on a room. Unless your parents want their own place."

"You'd be willing to have another woman in your house, love?"

"Whatever makes you happy. Besides, I can learn a lot from your mum."

"We'll discuss their wishes and make a decision that suits us all. How does that sound?"

"Like a perfect plan."

He kissed her soundly. "Can this day get any better?"

Fiona took his hand and laid it against her belly. "Yes, it can."

His eyes widened, then filled with tears. "You're with child?"

The door closed with a quiet thump, as Seamus departed giving them privacy. She and Keegan couldn't ask for better friends. She brushed a kiss on his cheek, her own eyes prickling. "You're to be a da again in January. Think you're up to three children?"

"I'll take as many as God gives us." He nuzzled her neck.

She shivered. His touch never ceased to affect her. "Looks like we'll be building on more than one room."

He threw back his head and guffawed. "We'll start first thing tomorrow."

THE END

What did you think of *A Bride for Keegan?*

Thank you so much for purchasing *A Bride for Keegan*. You could have selected any number of books to read, but you chose this book.

I hope it added encouragement and exhortation to your life. If so, it would be nice if you could share this book with your family and friends by posting to Facebook (www.facebook.com), Twitter (www.twitter.com), MeWe (www.mewe.com), Instagram (www.instagram.com) or other social networking site.

If you enjoyed this book and found some benefit in reading it, I'd appreciate it if you could take some time to post a review on Amazon, Goodreads, BookBub, or other book review site of your choice. Your feedback and support will help me to improve my writing craft for future projects and make this book even better.

Thank you again for your purchase.

Blessings,
Linda Shenton Matchett

P.S.: I hope you'll stop by my blog located on my website at http://www.LindaShentonMatchett.com. Or sign up to receive my monthly newsletter that contains book reviews, historical tidbits, sales, freebies, and new release information:
https://mailchi.mp/74bb7b34c9c2/lindashentonmatchettnewsletter

A Bride for Keegan

Acknowledgments

Although writing a book is a solitary task, it is not a solitary journey. There have been many who have helped and encouraged me along the way.

My parents, Richard and Jean Shenton, who presented me with my first writing tablet and encouraged me to capture my imagination with words. Thanks, Mom and Dad!

Scribes212 – my ACFW online critique group: Valerie Goree, Marcia Lahti, and the late Loretta Boyett (passed on to Glory, but never forgotten). Without your input, my writing would not be nearly as effective.

Eva Marie Everson – my mentor/instructor with Christian Writers' Guild. You took a timid, untrained student and turned her into a writer. Many thanks!

SincNE, and the folks who coordinate the Crimebake Writing Conference. I have attended many writing conferences, but without a doubt, Crimebake is one of the best. The workshops, seminars, panels, critiques, and every tiny aspect are well-executed, professional, and educational.

Special thanks to Hank Phillippi Ryan, Halle Ephron, and Roberta Isleib for your encouragement and spot-on critiques of my work.

Thanks to my Book Brigade who provide information, encouragement, and support.

Paula Proofreader (https://paulaproofreader.wixsite.com/home): I'm so glad I found you! My work is cleaner because of your eagle eye. Any mistakes are completely mine.

A heartfelt thank you to my brothers, Jack Shenton and Douglas Shenton, and my sister, Susan Shenton Greger for being enthusiastic cheerleaders during my writing journey. Your support means more than you'll know.

My husband, Wes, deserves special kudos for understanding my need to write. Thank you for creating my writing room – it's perfect, and I'm thankful for it every day. Thank you for your willingness to accept a house that's a bit cluttered, laundry that's not always done, and meals on the go. I love you.

And finally, to God be the glory. I thank Him for giving me the gift of writing and the inspiration to tell stories that shine the light on His goodness and mercy.

Want more Proxy Bride Romance? Read on for the first chapter in *A Bride for Seamus*.

Chapter One

White-hot shards of pain shot up Seamus Fitzpatrick's back, and he sucked in his breath, fighting the dizziness that threatened to topple him facedown into the dirt. With one hand on the horse's bridle, he bent over and whipped his handkerchief out of his pocket. Blotting at the perspiration streaming down his face, he waited for his vision to quit swimming.

The midday sun heated his shoulders under his cotton shirt while, Bess, the mare he'd purchased a couple of weeks ago, stood patiently by his side, seeming content to take a break from plowing. Seamus's head cleared, and he eased himself into an upright position. The muscles along his spine ached with a dull throb, but the piercing agony was gone. He blew out a deep breath and took a tentative step forward. Good. The ache was manageable. Doc Abbott had warned him the bullet that remained lodged in his body might never work its way out, and he'd suffer these episodes the rest of his life.

He'd prayed often for God to take care of the problem, but apparently He had other plans, and like the Apostle Paul, Seamus was destined to bear a constant thorn of the flesh. He wasn't enough of a Bible student to know if Paul's thorn was a physical ailment, but the man's writings were a balm on the worst days. Especially when his brother had an episode or his niece and nephew were cantankerous.

Bess nickered, then snorted and bobbed her head.

"Sorry, girl. I'm woolgathering. Sure, and we've got too many acres to prepare for planting for me to be turning my attention elsewhere." A hawk swooped in the cloudless sky overhead. A gorgeous day for sitting on the porch and putting up his feet. As if that were even possible. Numerous responsibilities awaited him inside as well, but with any luck the mail-order bride who'd arrived on last Saturday's train was doing something other than complaining.

He frowned and stuffed his handkerchief into his pocket. The third prospect in nine months, she'd responded to his ad in one of the eastern papers. After exchanging a handful of letters, he proposed she come to Iowa and meet him and the family before deciding if she wanted to marry. He'd been candid about the state of affairs, since the first two brides had informed him they never would have agreed to consider marrying him if they'd known about his brother. But in the few days since Julia Caron arrived, she'd caused dissension between the kids, frightened his brother on more than one occasion, and criticized the house and its contents. Her beauty appeared to be only skin deep. She cooked well enough, and her skills with a needle were exemplary, but those didn't make up for the spirit of unrest she'd brought with her.

A shriek sounded from the house, then shouting, and Seamus's gaze shot in that direction. Julia and Conor stormed out of the house. She pointed her finger in his brother's face, her lips curled in a sneer. He couldn't hear her words, but her attitude was clear enough from her expression. Something had happened between the two of them. Again.

Conor's face looked mulish, but he didn't respond, just stood in the yard with his arms crossed and his head shaking back and forth like a bull presented with a red cape. The woman finished her tirade, then marched back inside, slamming the door.

"Something's got to change, Bess." Seamus unhooked the mare from the plow and swung up onto her back. He turned her toward the house and gave her sides a gentle squeeze with his knees. With a whinny, she broke into a trot. "I know. Not what you had planned. Me neither."

He stopped the horse in the yard, slid from her back, and wrapped the reins over the porch railing. "Conor, what's going on?"

"I didn't do nuthin'." Conor scowled and headed to the barn.

"That's not what I asked...oh, never mind." Seamus stepped onto the porch and reached for the knob but missed as the door was flung open from inside.

Satchel in hand, Julia glowered at him. "I'm leaving. I've had enough. You'd better get used to being single, Mr. Fitzpatrick, because no woman in her right mind is going to take on this family. Your brother needs to be in an institution, and the children need a firm hand. You are too lenient with them, and they balk at any sort of discipline. I believe there is a three o'clock train, and I'd like to be on it."

"Miss Caron—"

"I've made up my mind, so don't ask me to stay." She looked down her nose at him, her lips nearly disappearing.

"I'm not. I was going to apologize that this...uh, arrangement didn't work out, and I'll hook Bess to the wagon as soon as I wash up."

"Oh." Her face reddened, and she had the decency to look abashed.

"Or I'd be happy to put you up in the hotel in town if you want to stay and try to find yourself another groom."

"No, thank you. I'd like to go home, if you please."

"Yes, ma'am." He took the bag from her and gestured to the rocking chair. "Why don't you have a seat, and I'll be ready in a jiffy."

She lowered herself in the chair and wrapped her arms around her middle, staring into the distance.

He studied her for a long moment, then descended the stairs and grabbed Bess's halter. He led her to the barn and hooked her to buckboard while his brother mucked one of the stalls. Conor must be fired up. He rarely took the initiative to clean out the barn. "She's leaving. I'll be back in a couple of hours. Will you be okay while I'm gone?"

"Yeah." Conor leaned on the shovel. "This is my fault, isn't it?"

"No. She's not a fit for lots of reasons." He clapped his brother on the shoulder. "God will send someone, Conor. You'll see."

"If you say so."

Seamus stifled a sigh. He wasn't convinced, but Conor didn't deserve to feel bad for the woman's departure. He climbed onto the wagon and drove it to the front of the house. Minutes later he was back on board having loaded her bag and trunk and taken a quick sponge bath. The ride to the station seemed interminable, but they managed to get there without incident. He paid for her ticket and gave her additional cash to assuage his guilt over the relief of seeing her go. Would God truly send someone, or was he kidding himself to believe there was a woman somewhere who would love their family such as it was?

Other Titles
Romance

Love's Harvest, Wartime Brides, Book 1

Love's Rescue, Wartime Brides, Book 2

Love's Belief, Wartime Brides, Book 3

Love's Allegiance, Wartime Brides, Book 4

Love Found in Sherwood Forest

A Love Not Forgotten

On the Rails

A Doctor in the House

Spies & Sweethearts, Sisters in Service, Book 1

The Mechanic & the MD, Sisters in Service, Book 2

The Widow & the War Correspondent, Sisters in Service, Book 3

Dinah's Dilemma (Westward Home and Hearts Mail-Order Brides, 10)

Rayne's Redemption (Westward Home & Hearts Mail-Order Brides, 15)

Legacy of Love (Keepers of the Light, Book 10)

Gold Rush Bride Hannah (Gold Rush Brides, Book 1)

Gold Rush Bride Caroline (Gold Rush Brides, Book 2)

Mystery

Under Fire, Ruth Brown Mystery Series, Book 1

Under Ground, Ruth Brown Mystery Series, Book 2

Under Cover, Ruth Brown Mystery Series, Book 3

Murder of Convenience, Women of Courage, Book 1

A Bride for Keegan

Murder at Madison Square Garden, Women of Courage, Book 2

Non-Fiction
WWII Word Find, Volume 1